# The Sherlock Holmes Seminars

## Volume 2

Produced by

**Thomas W. Campbell**

Thomas W. Campbell produced this book, using software tools to assist with spelling, grammar, sentence restructuring, rephrasing, and research — all in pursuit of historical and literary authenticity.



**The Sherlock Holmes Seminars**
**Volume 2**

First Edition: May 1, 2026
ISBN: 979-8-234-05535-4

Published in the United States of America by
The Sherlock Holmes Society USA

**www.SherlockHolmesSociety.com**

To contact the Publisher or Author:

**SherlockHolmesSociety@gmail.com**

221B
Sherlock Holmes Society USA

# Dedication

For the Sherlockians — you know who you are, and you know what you mean to me. This book would not exist without the warmth, wit, and wisdom of the remarkable community that has gathered around the legacy of Sherlock Holmes. In particular, the members of The Sherlock Holmes Society of the Cape Fear have been my companions on this journey from the very beginning. Our monthly meetings — part lively debate, part celebration, entirely wonderful — have given me more inspiration and encouragement than I can easily put into words. You have reminded me, again and again, why the Great Detective continues to matter, and why the friendships formed in his name are friendships worth treasuring.

- Thomas W. Campbell

# Author's Note

The Sherlock Holmes Seminars depicted in this book are not real — they never happened. The transcripts in this book are built around a single question:

### What if they had actually occurred?

What follows is a portrait of a seminar series as it might have unfolded, had The Strand Magazine elected to honor the Holmes stories in precisely this fashion.

But while these seminars were a product of the author's imagination, they are based on fact. The British Museum's Meeting Room is real. The year is 1900, and the public's grief over Sherlock Holmes — lost at Reichenbach Falls — still exists. Herbert Greenhough Smith was a genuine and accomplished figure, and the long standing literary editor of The Strand. Arthur Conan Doyle was very much alive in 1900, the man who had shaped Dr. Watson's raw notes and memories into the elegant narratives that captivated readers across the globe. And Dr. John H. Watson himself — retired army surgeon, London resident, and the tireless chronicler whose record-keeping gave these stories their existence — had by 1900 become as recognizable to the reading public as any living figure in England.

By 1900, only twenty-six Holmes stories had seen publication. These tales would come to be revered as *The Canon* — the definitive and authoritative body of Holmes literature. Although the seminars imagined in these pages never took place, they remain faithful to *The Canon.* Every detail and discussion that follows remains faithful to the facts as Dr. Watson recorded them and Conan Doyle presented them to the world.

This book is **VOLUME 2**, which includes transcripts of the imagined seminars covering all twelve stories found in The Memoirs of Sherlock Holmes.

# Table of Contents

# The Sherlock Holmes Seminars

To mark the dawn of the year 1900, *The Strand* conceived and organized an ambitious series of twenty-six public seminars, each devoted entirely to the close discussion of a single Sherlock Holmes story as written by Mr. Arthur Conan Doyle. What followed was thirteen weeks of Saturday and Sunday gatherings — interrupted only when a weekend coincided with a public holiday — that together formed one of the most remarkable literary events the new century had yet witnessed.

The seminars were held in a gracious meeting room made available by the British Museum in Bloomsbury, that great temple of knowledge and culture whose very atmosphere seemed ideally suited to the serious examination of great stories. Admission to each seminar was offered entirely free of charge, as *The Strand* was determined that no member of the public should be turned away on account of financial circumstance. However, as seating in the meeting room was necessarily limited, all those wishing to attend were required to register in advance directly with *The Strand Magazine*, ensuring that every chair was filled by an eager and prepared participant.

Presiding over each seminar as Moderator was Mr. Herbert Greenhough Smith, *The Strand Magazine's* distinguished editor, whose deep familiarity with the Holmes stories and whose gifts as a conversationalist made him the natural and ideal choice to guide each discussion. Seated permanently at the panel table alongside Mr. Greenhough Smith throughout the entire series were two gentlemen uniquely qualified to speak to the stories in question: Mr. Arthur Conan Doyle himself, the celebrated author who breathed life into every character and adventure under discussion, and his friend and collaborator, Dr. John H. Watson, whose own first-hand accounts of Mr. Holmes's cases form the very foundation of the canon. Their presence together at the panel table — author and chronicler side by side — lent the seminars an air of authority and intimacy that no reader of the stories could fail to appreciate.

Beyond these two permanent panelists, *The Strand* extended invitations to additional participants whose connection to each individual story made their presence especially valuable. Characters who had figured prominently in a given adventure — clients, witnesses, investigators, and others — were invited to join the panel for the seminar devoted to that story, offering perspectives and recollections that no author's pen, however skilled, could entirely capture on the page. The result was a series of discussions that moved fluidly between the literary and the personal, between craft and lived experience.

Convinced that the discussions taking place in that Bloomsbury meeting room deserved to be preserved and shared with the widest possible audience, The Strand Magazine engaged a team of professional stenographers to attend every seminar. What appears in these pages is an edited sample of each session. The full and unedited transcripts are retained by The Strand Magazine for posterity.

This book is **VOLUME 2**, which contains the edited transcripts of the seminars devoted to the following stories:

- *Silver Blaze*
- *The Cardboard Box*
- *The Yellow Face*
- *The Stock Broker's Clerk*
- *The Gloria Scott*
- *The Musgrave Ritual*
- *The Reigate Puzzle*
- *The Crooked Man*
- *The Resident Patient*
- *The Greek Interpreter*
- *The Naval Treaty*
- *The Final Problem*

# Silver Blaze

*First Published in December, 1892*
*Sponsored by The Strand Magazine*
*Meeting Room B, British Museum, London*

## The Fifteenth Seminar

**Herbert Greenhough Smith** — The Strand Editor & Moderator
**Arthur Conan Doyle** — Author and Watson's Literary Agent
**Dr. John H. Watson** —Colleague and Biographer of Sherlock Holmes
**Colonel Ross** — Owner of Silver Blaze
**Mr. Silas Brown** — Head Trainer, Mapleton Stables
**Mr. Ned Hunter** — Stable Lad, King's Pyland

Seminar Transcript

**SMITH**: Good evening, ladies and gentlemen, and welcome once more to what has become, I daresay, one of the more beloved Saturday institutions in London. We are fifteen seminars into our series, and I confess that this evening's story was one I anticipated above almost all the others. "Silver Blaze" is, in the estimation of many readers and critics, the finest of all the Holmes stories — a judgment with which I suspect our author may wish to quarrel, and which I look forward to testing. Gentlemen, welcome, all of you. Arthur, Dr. Watson — familiar faces to our audience by now. And to our guests this evening: Colonel Ross, Mr. Silas Brown, Mr. Ned Hunter — I thank you most sincerely for making the journey from the West Country.

**DOYLE**: The pleasure is ours, Smith. I confess, each seminar I come prepared to feel a faint embarrassment at hearing my own words read back to me, and each seminar I find myself caught up in spite of myself. Though I shall admit that "Silver Blaze" does occupy a particular corner of my affections.

**WATSON**: As it does mine — though perhaps for reasons that will become apparent as the evening proceeds. It was a case that took Holmes and me far out of our usual haunts, and the Dartmoor air, bracing as it was, did not prevent either of us from finding the whole business deeply unsettling before it was resolved.

**COLONEL ROSS**: Unsettling, Doctor, is a considerable understatement from where I stood. I lost my trainer, my horse was missing, and I had an audience of press and sporting men watching every move I made. I was not, at the time, in the best temper for the company of consulting detectives.

*Polite laughter from the audience*

**BROWN**: I would prefer not to revisit the week in question at all, Mr. Smith, but I gave my word to the Colonel and to The Strand, and I am not a man who breaks his word a second time.

*A quiet but significant murmur from the audience.*
*Mr. Brown shifts in his chair but does not look away*

**HUNTER**: I'll say my piece readily enough. Some of it's still a shame to me — but Mr. Holmes was fair about it, and I reckon I owe the same.

**SMITH**: Splendidly said, all of you. Let us begin, then, at the beginning. Colonel Ross, would you set the scene for us? Silver Blaze was, at the time, among the most celebrated racehorses in England. Describe, if you will, the situation at King's Pyland in the days before the crime.

**COLONEL ROSS**: Silver Blaze was the favorite for the Wessex Cup — a race of considerable importance and one I had every expectation of winning. My trainer, John Straker, had been in my employ for many years; I trusted him entirely and had no cause to doubt his management of the stables. King's Pyland is an isolated establishment on the edge of Dartmoor — deliberately so, for when a horse is as celebrated as Silver Blaze, you do not wish him to be easily accessible to strangers with mischief in mind. Straker was attentive to security, or so I believed. He kept his stable lads on short rations of liberty, and a watch was always set at night.

**SMITH**: Mr. Hunter — you were that watch on the fatal night. What can you tell us of the hours before you discovered that both Straker and the horse were gone?

**HUNTER**: I had the evening duty, sir. I was to stay up and keep my eye on the stable — that was regular. Around ten o'clock, a stranger came to the gate. Offered me money — quite a sum — to tell him about Silver Blaze's condition and training times. I sent him off sharply, I did. Then I went back to my supper, which Edith — that's one of the housemaids — had kept warm for me. Curried mutton, it was. After I ate, I... that is, I fell asleep. Not through any lack of diligence, I want it understood — something was wrong with the food. I was out for hours. When I woke, it was gone three in the morning. Straker's coat was on the hook; he'd gone out in the night. And the loose box was empty.

**SMITH**: Arthur — at this point in the story, Holmes and Watson are summoned to Dartmoor. What were the clues that drew Holmes's attention even before he left Baker Street?

**DOYLE**: The telegram from the Colonel, the reports in the papers, and — most critically — the absence of certain expected events. Holmes was particularly struck by the behavior of the dog. There was a trained dog at King's Pyland, and that dog had made no sound during the night. This, to Holmes, was the key that unlocked the whole affair. The intruder was known to the dog. And therefore known to the stable.

**WATSON**: I recall Holmes becoming rather animated about that point on the train down. I had dismissed the dog's silence as meaning nothing had occurred worth barking at — a thief would have been announced by the animal. Holmes corrected me. He said that the absence of the bark was itself the event. I confess I did not immediately understand him.

**DOYLE**: And when you arrived at King's Pyland, Watson?

**WATSON**: The scene was distressing. Straker's body had been found some distance from the stables, on the moor, with a severe head wound. And Silver Blaze — the most famous horse in England at that moment — had vanished completely.

**SMITH**: Mr. Hunter, you have alluded to something being wrong with your food. Holmes quickly identified opium as the agent, administered in the curry where its flavor could be disguised. Do you know who was responsible for that?

**HUNTER**: I do now, sir. I was pretty sure it was Mr. Fitzroy Simmons, the man who asked about Silver Blaze. But thanks to Mr. Holmes, it was actually Mr. Straker himself. Of course, I didn't see him do it. The whole business made me feel a proper fool — an experienced stable lad, drugged at his own supper, and by the very man I worked for.

**WATSON**: You ought not to judge yourself too harshly, Hunter. Opium in a strong curry is a devilishly difficult thing to detect. The alkaloid loses itself entirely in the spices. Holmes confirmed the quantity administered was sufficient to fell a man in thirty minutes — you had no chance of staying awake.

**HUNTER**: Generous of you, Doctor. But it's still a sore memory.

**SMITH**: Colonel Ross — when you first learned of Simpson's visit to the stable, did you believe him to be the murderer of Straker and the thief of your horse?

**COLONEL ROSS**: Like young Ned, I was certain of it. Or very nearly certain. The evidence seemed to point his way — he had a cravat found at the scene, he had motive in the form of gambling interests, and he'd been lurking about the neighborhood. Inspector Gregory was inclined the same way. We both thought Holmes would simply confirm what we suspected and Simpson would hang for it.

**DOYLE**: Which is, of course, a rather serviceable illustration of the danger of forming a theory before one possesses all the facts. Holmes refused to be drawn into that conclusion. He examined the cravat, he examined the mud around the stable, and he conducted a very particular inquiry into the mutton — which told him that Simpson had been at the kitchen, yes, but at the kitchen door, not inside the stable. The horse, Holmes noted, had been led out of the stable by Straker after the stable boy had fallen asleep.

**SMITH**: This brings us, gentlemen, to the most striking revelation of the whole case — the character of John Straker and what he intended to do the night he died. Arthur, would you take us through Holmes's reasoning?

**DOYLE**: Willingly. Holmes found, in Straker's private pocket-book, a bill from a London milliner — a dressmaker of some expense — made out to a "Mrs. Darbyshire," a woman whom the real Mrs. Straker knew nothing about. Straker had, in short, a second establishment to maintain and debts to hide. He required money and could not easily obtain it through honest means. He had, therefore, devised a scheme of astonishing — I would almost say audacious — cunning. He intended to lame Silver Blaze.

**COLONEL ROSS**: My own trainer. The man I trusted above all others with the care of the finest horse I have ever owned.

**DOYLE**: Indeed. And his method was equally sophisticated. Among his belongings was a very delicate surgical instrument — a cataract knife, used ordinarily in eye surgery for its extreme fineness of blade. Straker intended to make a small, near-invisible nick in the tendons of one of the horse's near legs — not enough to permanently injure the animal, but sufficient to produce a mysterious lameness on race day. He had placed a large bet, through an intermediary, against Silver Blaze. The horse would fail to perform; Straker would collect handsomely; no one would think to blame the trainer.

**WATSON**: The wickedness of it is compounded by its cleverness. A trainer explaining a horse's lameness as the result of some unknown injury on the moor — it would have been perfectly plausible. These things happen.

**SMITH**: But something went wrong. What happened on the moor that night?

**DOYLE**: Holmes reconstructed it thus: Straker led Silver Blaze away from the stable in the small hours, intending to perform the operation where no one would see. But when the moment came to apply the knife — and a horse, even a gentle one, will react sharply to the bite of a blade against its leg — Silver Blaze lashed out. The blow from an unshod hoof struck Straker in the head. He died almost instantly. Silver Blaze, now free and frightened, ran into the night.

**COLONEL ROSS**: Holmes told me this and I did not wish to believe it. A man I had trusted for years — conspiring against my horse, against me. And then killed by the very animal he meant to injure. There is something almost Biblical in it, I suppose.

**WATSON**: Holmes was careful to point out that Straker was not a cruel man in the conventional sense — merely a desperate one. The trap he had set for himself was one he had constructed entirely alone. His duplicity was the cause of his own death.

**HUNTER**: I won't pretend I was sorry for him, knowing what he'd intended. But I was sorry for Mrs. Straker, who knew nothing of the other woman or the scheme. She'd trusted him too.

**SMITH**: Mr. Brown — we come now to your part in the affair, which is in some ways the most delicate. Silver Blaze had fled the moor. Where did he go, and how did you come to find him?

**BROWN**: He came to us. Mapleton stable, which I managed for Lord Backwater, is not two miles from King's Pyland across the moor. In the early hours — while it was still dark — I discovered Silver Blaze wandering on the moor. Thoroughly frightened, sweating, but not injured. Recognising the horse — his markings are unmistakeable — I made a decision that I am not proud of, and which I have since paid for in full measure of embarrassment.

**SMITH**: You concealed him.

**BROWN**: I did. Silver Blaze was Lord Backwater's great rival for the Wessex Cup. With Silver Blaze out of the way — hidden — our own entry, Desborough, stood to win. I told myself it was only for the race. That I would see the horse returned afterwards. I made certain changes to his appearance — I will not go into the precise details — so that he would not be readily identified if anyone came looking. I kept him in a far paddock under a different name on the stable list.

**COLONEL ROSS**: I confess I could have cheerfully throttled Brown when Holmes revealed what he had done. Cheerfully and at length.

**BROWN**: I don't blame you, Colonel. I do not ask for your forgiveness — only to note that the horse was unharmed and that when Mr. Holmes presented me with the evidence of what he knew and made clear that cooperation was my only sensible path, I cooperated fully and immediately.

**SMITH**: Holmes's discovery of the horse at Mapleton — can you describe how he confronted you, Mr. Brown?

**BROWN**: He appeared at my yard with Watson one morning, cool as you like. He told me — and I mean he told me, not asked — that he knew I had Silver Blaze, that he knew what I had done with him, and that if I assisted him willingly, he would say nothing of my conduct to the police or to the press. He said the matter could be resolved quietly and that the Colonel would have his horse in time for the race. He was perfectly civil about it. Which somehow made it worse.

**WATSON**: Holmes had identified the Mapleton yard as the only possible location for the horse within a radius that a frightened animal could have covered on foot. He had also noticed, the previous day, certain marks in the turf near the paddock boundary that suggested recent activity and unusual disturbance.

**HUNTER**: I hadn't known that part of it until the story was printed. Brown keeping him all that time — it made my blood boil, I'll tell you. We were all in a wretched state at King's Pyland, not knowing if the horse was alive or dead, and there he was, eating good oats two miles away.

**BROWN**: He was very well cared for, Hunter. I want that on record. Whatever else I did, I did not neglect the horse.

*An uneasy silence falls briefly over the panel*

**SMITH**: Let the record show that Silver Blaze was indeed found in excellent health and condition. Colonel Ross, tell us how you found out that Silver Blaze had actually run in the Wessex Cup itself.

**COLONEL ROSS**: Holmes entered Silver Blaze in the race. Under a disguised name, with his appearance still altered — he had been painted or treated in some way to obscure his distinctive blaze, hence his name. I was furious, frankly. My horse had been missing for a week, I did not know for certain what had happened on the moor.

**WATSON**: I remember Holmes telling the Colonel that he was confident, and that the Colonel should trust him. Which is about as much as you ever get from Holmes when he has made up his mind.

**DOYLE**: And Silver Blaze won the Wessex Cup. Which is not quite the ending one expects from a story that began with a dead man on a moor.

**COLONEL ROSS**: He won it by half a length from Desborough. I watched from the rails not entirely certain which horse was mine. It was a peculiar experience. Holmes stood beside me — calm, amused, insufferably satisfied — and when the result was confirmed, he turned to me and said something about the sporting instincts of a great horse not being easily suppressed. I never entirely forgave him for the delay in identifying himself and his methods to me.

**DOYLE**: Holmes would argue, Colonel, that you had the horse and the result. He would say the method was his own private concern.

**COLONEL ROSS**: He would say exactly that. And it would be exactly as infuriating the second time as it was the first.

*The audience laughs warmly*

**SMITH**: I promised our audience that I would not let the evening pass without dwelling on what has already become, I believe, the most quoted exchange in the Holmes canon. Dr. Watson — you asked Holmes which incident he referred to as singular, did you not?

**WATSON**: I did. Holmes had observed that the dog at the stable was the curious incident. I pointed out that the dog had done nothing — there was nothing to observe. And Holmes replied that that was the curious incident.

**SMITH**: Arthur — when you wrote those lines, did you appreciate that you were creating what readers would call a definitive statement of Holmes's method?

**DOYLE**: I appreciated it in the moment — Watson's notes on the case contained precisely that exchange, and when I read it I set down my pen and thought: that is very good indeed. Whether it would survive the judgment of readers, one never knows in advance. I am gratified that it has. It is, I think, the purest expression of what separates Holmes from any ordinary investigator — the capacity to regard absence as data. Most minds catalogue what is present. Holmes catalogues what is missing, and weighs the two with equal care.

**COLONEL ROSS**: Which is all very well in a published story. In the middle of a crisis, it is considerably less comforting to be told that a dog's silence means your trusted trainer was a thief and a cheat.

**HUNTER**: There was another thing Mr. Holmes noticed that first day at King's Pyland that I've never seen printed. He looked at the feed bins very carefully — I was watching him as he walked round the stable, touching nothing, just looking. He told me afterward that the amounts of food remaining in the bins told him something about which of the horses had been disturbed during the night and which had not. He said that animals, like people, cannot sleep quietly when they are frightened, and that their appetite the following morning reflects it. I'd worked with horses fifteen years and I'd never thought of it quite that way.

**WATSON**: Holmes examines the world with a species of patience that I find simultaneously admirable and exhausting. He has explained to me on numerous occasions that the faculty of observation is not a gift but a discipline — that any person could achieve a measure of his results if they trained themselves to attend to the world around them with sustained care. I have tried. My results remain, I confess, modest.

**DOYLE**: Watson, you are considerably harder on yourself than the facts warrant.

**WATSON**: You are kind, Arthur. Holmes is considerably harder on me than you are, and I suspect his assessment is more accurate.

*General laughter*

**SMITH**: Gentlemen, we move toward our closing portion of the evening. I should like to give each of you a moment to reflect on what the case meant to you — not in terms of facts, but in terms of what it left behind. Colonel Ross, you first.

**COLONEL ROSS**: Silver Blaze raced for another three seasons after the Wessex Cup and won eight more times, including the Gold Cup at Ascot. He is retired now to my stud, and I expect he will sire fine horses for many years to come. As for what the case left behind — I think I am a more cautious man than I was. I trusted Straker absolutely, and that trust was betrayed in a way I would never have imagined. I engage my people on shorter terms now and examine the accounts more closely. Whether that is wisdom or merely suspicion, I could not say.

**BROWN**: I left Mapleton the season after the race. Lord Backwater was gracious about it — he had not been informed of what I did, and I told him before I left, which was, I think, the least I owed him. I work now for a smaller yard in Wiltshire and I have not placed a bet in three years. What I did was a form of theft, though no court would have named it so. I have made my peace with that in the only way available to me, which is by not doing anything of the kind again.

**HUNTER**: For me it's simpler. I had a good horse in my care and I failed to protect him through no fault of my own, but it still weighs on me. I keep a sharper eye on the feed now. And I've never touched curried mutton since.

*The audience responds with warmth and some laughter*

**WATSON**: The case stays with me for reasons that are partly professional and partly personal. The journey to Dartmoor — the open moor at twilight, the remoteness of King's Pyland, the peculiar atmosphere of a case played out against that landscape — it had a quality that few of our investigations have matched. And Holmes was at his best. Not showy — he was rarely showy when he was genuinely engaged — but deeply, quietly purposeful. I think of the Dartmoor case often when I try to explain to people what it means to watch him work. It is not the theatrical moments. It is the long silences, the careful looking, the refusal to be hurried by the pressure of events. That is the thing that is difficult to put into words, and which I hope I have managed, imperfectly, to record.

**DOYLE**: I wrote "Silver Blaze" under some pressure, as I recall — the monthly deadline is an unforgiving master, and I had not quite resolved in my own mind how the horse had come to be hidden at Mapleton when I sat down to begin. I confess that the story assembled itself around me as I wrote, which is more common an experience than I would like to admit to readers who expect authorial omniscience. The death of Straker was in my notes from Watson almost exactly as it appears in print. The dog, the cataract knife, the sheep — all of it was there. My contribution was principally the arrangement.

**SMITH**: Arthur, you are famously said to have grown somewhat weary of Holmes by the period in which this story was written — the early nineties. You killed him, after all, at the Reichenbach Falls the following year. Do you regret it?

**DOYLE**: I regret the fuss it caused. I have never quite regretted the decision, though public opinion has not been gentle with me on the subject. Holmes is, I confess, a more demanding character to write than any of the others I have attempted. He requires the author to be somewhat cleverer than comes naturally. I cannot write a Holmes story without the plot being genuinely solved in advance — the character will not sustain a swindle. Other characters might carry a narrative by charm or incident even if the plotting is imprecise. Holmes cannot. He demands rigour. And rigour, night after night with a deadline approaching, is fatiguing.

**WATSON**: I may observe, as someone who has lived in Holmes's company rather more literally than Arthur has, that rigor is indeed fatiguing. He can be an exceedingly difficult man to share rooms with. But there is no one on earth I would have wished beside me in the library at King's Pyland, or on that bleak moor, or at the rails watching Silver Blaze come in.

*Mr. Smith accepts several written questions passed forward from the assembled audience*

**SMITH**: I have just been handed several questions from the audience. A question for Dr. Watson: "Did Holmes ever express any sympathy for Straker, given the circumstances of his death?"

**WATSON**: He expressed — I would say — a clinical sympathy. He noted that Straker had been very clever in the planning of his scheme and very unlucky in its execution. Holmes does not often make moral pronouncements about the subjects of his investigations. He tends to confine himself to facts. But he said once, on the train back to London, that a man who had spent years in faithful service and destroyed it all in a week for the sake of a milliner's bill was a man deserving more pity than censure. Whether that constitutes sympathy, I leave to the audience to judge.

**SMITH**: A question for Colonel Ross: "Did you ever learn the identity of the gamblers for whom Fitzroy Simpson was acting as intermediary?"

**COLONEL ROSS**: Holmes gave me the name of one of them in confidence. I elected not to pursue the matter publicly — doing so would have opened the whole business to more press attention than it had already received, and I wished the affair to settle. The man in question suffered considerable financial loss when Silver Blaze won the Wessex Cup, which I found was a satisfactory form of justice.

**SMITH**: And a final question, addressed to Arthur: "Are there other cases from Dr. Watson's notes involving Silver Blaze or Colonel Ross that may be published in future?"

**DOYLE**: Watson has more notes than I have lifetimes to work through. Whether Silver Blaze features among the unpublished material I cannot say. I can say that the Colonel has been patient with me this evening, and that if there is a story in those files that reflects well on him, he shall have the right of first refusal on its accuracy before it goes to press.

**COLONEL ROSS**: That is the most sensible thing you have said all evening, Doyle.

*General laughter and sustained applause from the audience*

**SMITH**: Gentlemen, I am reluctant to bring this evening to a close, but the Museum's patience has limits, and I am mindful that several of our guests have trains to catch. Let me say on behalf of The Strand Magazine and on behalf of every person in this room how profoundly grateful we are for your candor, your good humor, and your willingness to revisit events that were, for some of you, painful in the extreme. "Silver Blaze" will endure, I am quite certain, long after all of us are gone from the scene — and this evening's conversation has given it new dimensions that even its original readers could not have imagined. Silver Blaze himself, we are told, grazes in pleasant retirement, and one trusts he is indifferent to the extent of his own fame. The rest of us, I think, are not quite so fortunate. Ladies and gentlemen, thank you. Good evening.

*Sustained applause*

# The Cardboard Box

*First Published in January, 1893*
*Sponsored by The Strand Magazine*
*Meeting Room B, British Museum, London*

**The Sixteenth Seminar**

**Herbert Greenhough Smith** — The Strand Editor & Moderator
**Arthur Conan Doyle** — Author and Watson's Literary Agent
**Dr. John H. Watson** —Colleague and Biographer of Sherlock Holmes
**Inspector Lestrade** —Scotland Yard Inspector
**Ms. Sarah Cushing** —Recipient of the two severed Ears
**Ms. Susan Cushing** —Sarah's Sister

Seminar Transcript

**SMITH:** Ladies and gentlemen, welcome to the sixteenth in our series of commemorative seminars, presented here in the public meeting room of the British Museum under the auspices of The Strand Magazine. I am Herbert Greenhough Smith, editor of that publication, and I have the honor once again of serving as your moderator. Joining me this afternoon are the two gentlemen whose names have become inseparable from the cases we discuss in this series. To my left, the author who gave these adventures their literary form, Arthur Conan Doyle. And beside him, the man who lived these events at first hand and furnished Arthur with the detailed case notes upon which each story rests, Dr. John H. Watson. Gentlemen, welcome.

**DOYLE:** It is always a pleasure, Smith.

**WATSON:** Indeed. Though I confess that the prospect of today's seminar touches me rather more keenly than most. The affair of the cardboard box is not one that a man easily forgets, and the presence of our guests this afternoon makes it all the more affecting.

**SMITH:** On that note, let me introduce those guests. We are joined today by three individuals whose roles in this singular case were as central as those of Holmes and Watson themselves. First, from Croydon, Miss Susan Cushing, the lady to whose door this grim affair was quite literally delivered. Miss Cushing, welcome.

**SUSAN CUSHING:** Thank you, Mr. Smith. I shall say only that I hope it may do some good, my coming here and speaking of it all again. It is not an experience one revisits willingly.

**SMITH:** We are most grateful for your courage in joining us. Second, Miss Sarah Cushing, the younger sister of Miss Susan Cushing. Miss Sarah Cushing, welcome.

**SARAH CUSHING:** I am here, Mr. Smith. I will say what needs to be said.

**SMITH:** And finally, a gentleman well known to this series, Inspector G. Lestrade of Scotland Yard, who conducted the official police investigation into this matter. Inspector Lestrade, welcome back.

**LESTRADE:** Much obliged, Mr. Smith. Always glad to assist the public's understanding of our work.

**SMITH:** Let us begin at the beginning, as it were. Miss Susan Cushing, the entire extraordinary business commenced when you received a parcel through the post. Would you describe for us what arrived and what you made of it?

**SUSAN CUSHING:** It was a cardboard box, Mr. Smith — a common enough thing in appearance, or so I thought. It had been posted from Belfast. The address was written in rough block letters. When I cut the string and opened it, I found inside the box a quantity of coarse salt, and packed within the salt — I shall never forget it so long as I live — two human ears. Severed. I screamed for Mrs. Hargrove next door, and Mrs. Hargrove sent for the police.

**SMITH:** A dreadful discovery, beyond question. Inspector Lestrade, you were among the first officers to attend. What were your initial impressions?

**LESTRADE:** My first impression, if I'm honest, was that it was some sort of a cruel prank by a medical student. We see that sort of thing from time to time. Parts preserved in salt, posted to innocent parties for the purpose of a fright. Miss Cushing is a respectable, retired lady with no obvious enemies, and the ears appeared to have been preserved with some degree of care. I was not immediately certain we were dealing with a murder. That said, I recognised that the matter warranted serious attention, and I therefore consulted Mr. Holmes.

**WATSON:** I recall that morning very well. Holmes and I arrived at Cross Street in Croydon and were admitted to Miss Cushing's sitting room. Holmes wasted no time in examining the box and its contents with his lens.

**DOYLE:** Watson's notes on Holmes's examination of the box are among the most precise in the entire collection of cases, and I have endeavored to render them faithfully. Holmes observed that the string with which the box had been tied was coarse, of a kind more commonly used aboard ship than in domestic or commercial settings, and that the knot with which it was fastened was what sailors call a reef knot — a detail that pointed unmistakably toward a seafaring individual as the sender.

**SMITH:** And the ears themselves conveyed meaning to Mr. Holmes beyond the obvious horror?

**WATSON:** They did. Holmes examined both ears with great care. One was a woman's ear — small, finely formed, with a piercing for an earring. The other was a man's ear, larger and differently shaped. He noted that the woman's ear had been preserved very recently and that the preservation was not that of a trained medical hand but of someone who had acquired a rough working knowledge of such things, again consistent with a sailor. And then Holmes said something that quite astonished me.

**SMITH:** What did he say?

**WATSON:** He said — and I am recalling his words as nearly as I can — that the woman's ear bore a striking similarity in its particular shape and formation to the ears of Miss Susan Cushing herself, seated before us. He said that such a resemblance between ears is a family trait, and that the ear belonged almost certainly to a near relative of Miss Cushing's.

**SUSAN CUSHING:** I remember it. I remember how he looked at me when he said it. It was as if the words came from somewhere very far away.

I had two sisters. I knew then, though I did not want to know, that the ear might belong to one of them.

**SMITH:** At that time, Miss Cushing, had you formed any hypothesis yourself as to why such a package might have been sent to you?

**SUSAN CUSHING:** I had not the faintest idea, Mr. Smith. I told Mr. Holmes as much. I said that I was a quiet woman, that I had lived peaceably in Croydon, and that I could not imagine any person bearing me sufficient ill will to send me such a thing. I had had some medical students as lodgers some years before and had been obliged to turn them out for their disorderly behavior, and I mentioned that to Mr. Holmes as a possible, if distant, explanation. But even I did not truly believe it.

**LESTRADE:** The medical student theory remained on the table for a brief while longer. When Holmes mentioned the lodgers to me I was prepared to pursue it. But Holmes had already moved ahead of that. He pressed Miss Cushing about her family circumstances.

**SMITH:** And it was in pressing into those family circumstances that the true thread of the matter began to reveal itself. Miss Cushing, you told Holmes about your sisters at that first interview?

**SUSAN CUSHING:** I told him that I had two sisters. That my younger sister Mary had married a man named Jim Browner, who was a steward on a Liverpool boat, and was living with him in Liverpool. And that my other sister, Sarah — who is here with us today — had until recently been lodging in Penton Street, Walworth. I had not been on comfortable terms with Sarah for some time.

**SMITH:** Miss Sarah Cushing, this is where your part in this story becomes rather unavoidable. Would you speak to what had occurred in the period leading up to these events?

**SARAH CUSHING:** I will speak plainly, Mr. Smith. Some two years before the box arrived, I had been staying with my sister Susan. While I was there, I made the acquaintance of Jim Browner and his friend Alec Fairbairn, both seafaring men. Jim Browner was at that time attentive to me. I will not deny that I thought something might come of it. But he turned his attention to Mary instead, and he married her. I was not — I was not well pleased by that. Fairbairn and I remained friends, and through me, Fairbairn came to know Mary.

**SMITH:** And that acquaintance between Fairbairn and Mary — what did it become?

**SARAH CUSHING:** It became something it ought not to have become. I will not pretend otherwise, not before this audience. Fairbairn was a man of easy address and Mary — Mary was not a steady woman. I had introduced them. That is my part in it and I have no means of escaping it.

**WATSON:** Holmes learned from Miss Susan Cushing that Jim Browner had become aware of the improper character of the connection between his wife Mary and Fairbairn, and that it had led to very great unhappiness in the household. Susan had spoken with Browner about it and had later quarreled with Sarah over the whole business. It was this quarrel that had estranged the two sisters.

**SMITH:** Inspector Lestrade, at what point did the investigation take on the character of a murder inquiry rather than a case of criminal mischief?

**LESTRADE:** Once Holmes established that the ear belonged to a relation of Miss Cushing's, and once we understood the connection between the two sisters, Mary's husband, and Fairbairn, I sent inquiries to Liverpool. Very quickly it became apparent that Mary Browner had not been seen for some time, and that Alec Fairbairn had also dropped out of sight. At that point we were dealing with a disappearance at minimum, and the evidence of those ears pointed to something considerably worse.

**DOYLE:** The narrative in the published story moves somewhat swiftly through the investigative middle portion, as Watson's notes necessarily compress certain procedural details. What the story conveys, I hope, is the inexorable logic by which Holmes arrived at his conclusions — that a sailor, made frantic by jealousy, had committed a double murder and had sent the trophies of that murder to the woman he held responsible for his wife's ruin.

**SARAH CUSHING:** That is the plain truth of it. The box was meant for me, Mr. Smith, not for Susan. The address on it was Miss S. Cushing, and Jim Browner intended it for Sarah Cushing of Walworth — for me. He blamed me, and rightly so in his mind, for bringing Fairbairn into Mary's life. He had my old address from some previous communication but used Susan's street instead of mine. That was the only reason Susan received it rather than I.

**SMITH:** That is a haunting detail, Miss Sarah Cushing. The wrong sister received the package intended to terrorize you.

**SARAH CUSHING:** It is. And when I understood what had happened — when I learned what was in that box and who it had been meant for — I cannot tell you the weight of it. I have carried it since.

**SMITH:** Inspector Lestrade, you eventually obtained a confession from Jim Browner. How did that come about?

**LESTRADE:** Browner made no great attempt to conceal himself once the inquiry closed in on him. He was apprehended aboard his vessel, the May Day. He was a broken man. The passion that had driven him to the act seemed to have burned itself out entirely and left only the ruin of a man behind. When I spoke to him, he confessed freely.

**WATSON:** His account as Holmes later conveyed it to me was very vivid. He had discovered that his wife Mary was to go out on the water with Fairbairn, and he followed them. He confronted them in the boat on the water, and — in a frenzy of jealous rage — he killed them both. He then cut off an ear from each of them, packed the ears in a box with coarse salt, and posted the box to what he believed was Sarah's address. After that he returned to his duties aboard the May Day, as if the demon had been exorcised by the act, though of course no such exorcism was possible.

**SMITH:** Arthur, when you came to write this story, was there any element of Browner's situation that you found yourself wrestling with in terms of how to render it?

**DOYLE:** The story raises, in a quiet way, questions that are not easily resolved. Browner was a man who had been genuinely wronged. His wife had been unfaithful to him, and the man who had entered his household and destroyed his marriage had done so without scruple. I do not say this to excuse what Browner did — he committed two murders and he would face the law's accounting for it. But Watson's notes made me feel, as I read them, the human tragedy at the heart of the case. Holmes himself, I believe, felt it. He uttered something to Watson at the close of the matter that touched on the misery of human life. I tried to convey that note of melancholy in the published version.

**WATSON:** He did feel it. I remember Holmes sitting quietly after we had heard the full account, and he spoke of what a dreadful thing it was that men and women could be brought to such ends. It was one of those moments when the purely analytical quality of his mind gave way to something rather more humane.

**SMITH:** Miss Susan Cushing, I wonder if you might share with us how you experienced the presence of Holmes during the investigation. You had, of course, no prior acquaintance with him.

**SUSAN CUSHING:** He is not a man one forgets, Mr. Smith. He said very little at our first meeting that could be called reassuring in the usual sense — he was not warm in the way a clergyman or a doctor might be warm. But there was about him a quality of complete attention that I found steadying. He looked at everything. He asked his questions precisely and waited for answers without hurrying them. When he told me that the woman's ear was very likely that of a close relative, and that I should be prepared for painful news, he said it directly, without cushioning it so much that the meaning was lost. I was grateful for that directness, even though it cost me something to hear it.

**SMITH:** And after the investigation concluded — after the truth of Mary's fate was established and Browner was taken — how did you find yourself?

**SUSAN CUSHING:** I found myself with one sister gone and the other greatly changed. The box came to me by mistake, but the grief that followed it was real enough and belonged entirely to our family. I returned to Croydon, to my house, to my sitting room, and I went on. There is not much more to say than that.

**SMITH:** Miss Sarah Cushing, I think I must ask you — and you are of course free to decline — whether you feel, looking back, that you bear a responsibility for what occurred.

**SARAH CUSHING:** I do not decline the question. I have asked it of myself every day since it all came out. I introduced Alec Fairbairn to Mary. I knew what Fairbairn was. I knew that Jim Browner was a man of strong feeling who had taken Mary's faithfulness as the foundation of his life. Did I introduce them out of spite — because Browner had chosen Mary over me? I have searched my conscience on that point and I cannot give you a comfortable answer. I believe there was something of that in it, though I did not say so to myself at the time. Mary is dead. Alec Fairbairn is dead. Jim Browner will answer for it before the law. And I live with my part in the matter. That is the situation.

**WATSON:** It takes some courage to say so, Miss Cushing.

**SARAH CUSHING:** Courage would have been acting differently to begin with, Dr. Watson.

**SMITH:** Inspector Lestrade, from a professional standpoint — the question of how Holmes was able to read the available evidence and arrive so quickly at a theory involving a sailor, a marital dispute, and a double homicide — does that still impress you, looking back?

**LESTRADE:** I will give Holmes his due, and I say this as a man who has worked alongside him on a good many cases and who does not always find his methods easy to follow. On this occasion he was ahead of Scotland Yard by a considerable distance and he was right. The detail of the knot in the string — that is the sort of thing my men might have noted and set aside as having no particular significance. Holmes fixed upon it immediately and drew from it the conclusion that led him to the seafaring connection and from there to Browner. The speed of it was remarkable. I said as much to him at the time, and he received the compliment with his usual equanimity, which is to say he did not receive it at all and simply moved on.

**DOYLE:** That is very like him, as Watson describes him. Holmes has no interest in admiration for its own sake. The problem is the thing — once it is resolved, his attention moves on. Watson has often noted that quality.

**WATSON:** It is perfectly true. Holmes himself once spoke of the work as its own reward, and I believe that was entirely sincere. He did not need the gratitude of those he helped, though it was sometimes offered. What he needed was the puzzle.

**SMITH:** As we draw this seminar toward its close, I should like to give each of our guests a final opportunity to address the audience directly on any point they wish. Miss Susan Cushing, perhaps you would begin?

**SUSAN CUSHING:** I came here today because I thought it right to come, not because it was easy. The story, as Arthur has written it, is accurate in its particulars as far as I can judge, and the events he describes did happen very much as he describes them. If there is anything I should wish the audience to take away, it is this: that these were not fictional people. Mary was my sister. She was a real woman who made poor choices and who died for it at the hands of a man driven beyond his reason by jealousy. Whatever her faults, she did not deserve what was done to her. I am glad she is remembered, even in this indirect fashion.

**SMITH:** Thank you, Miss Cushing. Miss Sarah Cushing?

**SARAH CUSHING:** I have nothing to add to what I have already said. The events are as they occurred. My part in them is as I have described it. I would only say to anyone who might find themselves in a position similar to mine — in possession of a grievance, and of the means to act upon it in some small, seemingly innocent way — that there are no innocent ways of acting upon grievance. What I set in motion had an ending I never foresaw and would never have wished. I do not say this for sympathy. I say it because it is true.

**SMITH:** Inspector Lestrade?

**LESTRADE:** Only that I should like the record to show that Scotland Yard conducted itself properly in this investigation, that we acted upon the evidence available to us at each stage, and that the formal arrest and charge of James Browner were carried out by my officers in an orderly fashion. Mr. Holmes's contribution was invaluable, as I have said. We have worked together on a number of cases and I have always found him, whatever his eccentricities, to be a man who serves the interests of justice. I should also like to say — since we are speaking frankly — that cases of this nature, involving crimes of domestic passion, are among the most difficult for any police force to navigate. The evidence does not present itself cleanly. The motive is not at once apparent from the outside. It requires the sort of reasoning from fine detail that is, frankly, not yet sufficiently practiced in our regular detective work, and I hope that cases such as this one, brought before a wider public, may in time contribute to changing that.

**SMITH:** That is a generous and thoughtful observation, Inspector. Dr. Watson, any final remarks?

**WATSON:** Only to say that of all the cases in which I accompanied Holmes, this is among those which most clearly demonstrates why I have always felt it worthwhile to set these adventures down as carefully as I could. The technical feat of reading the evidence — the knot, the string, the ears, the postmark — that is remarkable, as Lestrade says. But the human content of this case is equally remarkable. Here are four people — Jim Browner, Mary Browner, Alec Fairbairn, and Sarah Cushing — whose intersecting lives produced a catastrophe that left two of them dead and the others permanently altered. Holmes once said to me, as we sat together after this case was concluded, something to the effect that our world is a sad one. I believe this case illustrates precisely what he meant.

**SMITH:** Arthur?

**DOYLE:** I will say simply that I am grateful, as always, to Watson for the material with which he has trusted me, and grateful today to Miss Susan Cushing, Miss Sarah Cushing, and Inspector Lestrade for agreeing to speak with us. To write a story is one thing. To sit in a room with the people who lived it is quite another, and I find it — though I have now done so fifteen times before in this series — still remarkable. The Cardboard Box is not among the lighter tales in the collection. It is a story about jealousy and its consequences, about the way a single decision — or a series of small decisions — can produce an outcome that no one involved ever intended or desired. I am glad it has been discussed here today, and I am glad that the people at its centre have had the opportunity to speak for themselves.

**SMITH:** On behalf of The Strand Magazine and on behalf of this audience, I thank all of our participants. To Arthur Conan Doyle and Dr. John H. Watson, as ever, our deepest gratitude. To Inspector Lestrade, to Miss Susan Cushing, and to Miss Sarah Cushing: your candor, your composure, and your willingness to revisit these painful events in a public forum have been both illuminating and genuinely moving. Good afternoon.

*Sustained applause*

# The Yellow Face

*First Published in February, 1893*
*Sponsored by The Strand Magazine*
*Meeting Room B, British Museum, London*

## The Seventeenth Seminar

**Herbert Greenhough Smith** — The Strand Editor & Moderator
**Arthur Conan Doyle** — Author and Watson's Literary Agent
**Dr. John H. Watson** —Colleague and Biographer of Sherlock Holmes
**Mr. Grant Monroe** — Client of Mr. Sherlock Holmes
**Mrs. Effie Monroe** — Grant Monroe's Wife
**Ms. Lucy Monroe** — Grand & Effie's Daughter

### Seminar Transcript

**SMITH**: Good afternoon, ladies and gentlemen. Welcome to the seventeenth seminar in our series commemorating the cases of the celebrated Mr. Sherlock Holmes. My name is Herbert Greenhough Smith, editor of The Strand Magazine, and it is my privilege once again to serve as your moderator. We meet today in the public meeting room of the British Museum, and I can see from the audience before me that the interest in these gatherings has not diminished in the slightest since our series commenced. As always, I am joined by Arthur Conan Doyle, whose pen has rendered these remarkable adventures available to the reading public, and by Dr. John H. Watson, whose original notes and observations have formed the very bedrock upon which each story rests. Arthur, Dr. Watson, welcome.

**DOYLE**: Thank you, Smith. It is always a pleasure, and I confess that today's seminar is one I have anticipated with considerable feeling. The case we take up today is, in certain respects, an unusual one, and I am grateful that our guests have consented to join us.

**WATSON**: Indeed. I should say at once that there is a particular quality to this case which distinguishes it from most of the others we have discussed in this series, and I suspect that quality will make itself evident before very long.

**SMITH**: I have no doubt it will, Doctor. Before we proceed to our guests, I wonder if you might both offer a brief word by way of introduction to the story itself. Arthur, would you begin?

**DOYLE**: Gladly. The case which Watson furnished to me under the title "The Yellow Face" is set in Norbury, a suburb south of London, and concerns a gentleman named Grant Monroe, who came to consult Mr. Holmes under circumstances that had caused him very great unease. Mr. Monroe was a hop merchant, and by all accounts a man of straightforward and honorable character. He had been married to his wife, Effie, for some years, and had considered their domestic life a thoroughly happy one—until, without apparent explanation, a change came over his wife's conduct that left him bewildered and alarmed.

**WATSON**: I can add a little color to that, if I may. Holmes and I received Mr. Monroe at Baker Street. I recall that Holmes, before the man had said scarcely a word, made several deductions from his physical appearance—his pipe, the state of his hands, and so forth. The case that Mr. Monroe laid before Holmes was, in its essentials, this: his wife had begun making secret visits to a small cottage near their home, a cottage that had lately been let by a newcomer to the neighborhood. She had on one occasion asked him for a considerable sum of money—one hundred pounds—without offering any account of what it was for. And when Mr. Monroe had approached the cottage window one evening, he had seen a face looking out at him—a face that he described as yellow in complexion, fixed, and strange, almost as though it were not quite human.

**SMITH**: A disturbing series of events by any measure. Now, it is my very great pleasure to introduce our three guests today, all of them members of the same family, all of them bearing directly upon the events of this case. Mr. Grant Monroe, Mrs. Effie Monroe, and Miss Lucy Monroe. Mr. Monroe, Mrs. Monroe, Miss Monroe, welcome, and thank you for making the journey to be with us.

**GRANT MONROE**: Thank you, Mr. Smith. I shall admit that I did not accept the invitation of The Strand immediately or without some hesitation. These are personal matters, and matters in which I do not present myself in an entirely flattering light. But my wife persuaded me that it might do some good, both for the readers of The Strand and perhaps for ourselves, to speak openly about what occurred.

**EFFIE MONROE**: And I am grateful to my husband for agreeing. I would not have insisted, but I did feel it strongly. We have had such peace in our household since everything came to light that I am no longer afraid to speak of it—not even before an audience such as this.

**SMITH**: And Miss Lucy?

**LUCY MONROE**: I am glad to be here, sir.

**SMITH**: Capital. Then let us begin at what I think must be the natural beginning. Mr. Monroe, the story as published opens with you, so to speak. You arrived at Baker Street to consult Mr. Holmes. What was it that finally drove you to seek his help? Clearly things had been troubling you for some time before you made that journey.

**GRANT MONROE**: They had, yes. You must understand that I am not, by temperament, a suspicious man. I had always trusted Effie entirely. Our marriage had been, as far as I knew, a source of mutual happiness and comfort. She is an American by birth—from Atlanta, in Georgia—and came to England some years before we met. She had been widowed before our marriage; her first husband, a Mr. John Hebron, had died of yellow fever not long before she settled here. I knew this. She had told me. And knowing it, I thought I understood her entirely.

**SMITH**: And then things changed.

**GRANT MONROE**: Then things changed. The cottage near our home—it had been empty for some time, and then it was let. Not long after that, Effie began making excuses to go out. I might not have remarked upon it at all, except that on one occasion I happened to follow her, and I saw her enter that cottage. She stayed perhaps half an hour and then came out. She said nothing of it to me. A day or two later, she asked me for one hundred pounds. She was not extravagant by nature; this was an extraordinary request. She would give me no reason for it, except to say that she could not explain, that I must trust her, and that it would be better for both of us if I asked no further questions. I was struck dumb by it.

**WATSON**: If I may, Mr. Monroe—when you came to Baker Street, you were in a very agitated state. I remarked upon it at the time in my notes. Holmes was struck by certain signs in your appearance. You had been so absorbed in your troubles, I think, that you had let your pipe go cold in your pocket without noticing.

**GRANT MONROE**: Yes, so Mr. Holmes observed, very much to my surprise. I cannot say that the accuracy of his observation did a great deal to settle my nerves. One does not expect a man to read one quite so clearly from the state of one's tobacco pouch.

**DOYLE**: That, I believe, was one of Holmes's particular pleasures—the initial reading of a new client. Watson's notes were always quite vivid on those moments.

**WATSON**: They were moments Holmes relished, I think. He could seldom resist them.

**SMITH**: Mrs. Monroe, I want to ask you directly about your own position throughout this period. Your husband was in a state of considerable distress. You were keeping a secret from him. That must have been a very great strain.

**EFFIE MONROE**: It was the most difficult period of my life—and I say that as a woman who has known real grief. When my first husband died, I believed that part of my life was simply over. I had Lucy, but I did not believe I could give her a settled home in England; I had very little money, and circumstances were such that I placed her in the care of a woman in America while I came to England to find my footing. In time, I met Grant. We were married. And then—some time after our marriage—I was contacted. I learned that the woman who had been caring for Lucy could no longer do so, and that Lucy herself was asking for me.

**SMITH**: And so you arranged to bring Lucy to England.

**EFFIE MONROE**: I brought Lucy to England and installed her, with a care giver, in the cottage nearby. I could not bear to have her farther away. And yet—and yet I was afraid to tell Grant. I was afraid of what the revelation might mean for our marriage, for our life together. I asked him for the money to maintain the cottage and the woman who was living there with Lucy and looking after her. I could not explain why without explaining everything. So I asked him to trust me. I know now how that must have appeared to him.

**GRANT MONROE**: It appeared, I am afraid to say, as though there were something clandestine and troubling going on. A secret I was not to be permitted to know. I do not blame Effie for fearing how I might receive the truth. But at the time I was simply at a loss.

**SMITH**: Dr. Watson, let me bring you in here. When Mr. Monroe described the yellow face at the window of the cottage—that detail was clearly central to Holmes's thinking. What was Holmes's reading of it at the time?

**WATSON**: Holmes was, I must say, quite fascinated by that detail. A face at the window—rigid, yellow-hued, expressionless, or nearly so. He formed a view about it, as he always did. He concluded that it was likely a mask of some kind, though he did not say so explicitly to Mr. Monroe at the time. His overall reading of the case was that Mrs. Monroe was being subjected to some form of pressure—that there was a figure in that cottage who held some claim over her, possibly connected to her life before her marriage to Mr. Monroe.

**DOYLE**: Holmes speculated, as Watson's notes record, along quite specific lines. He supposed that Effie's former life in America might have produced complications that had followed her to England. That the person in the cottage might be someone she had known before, and that the money she had requested from her husband was being paid, in essence, to secure that person's silence.

**WATSON**: He laid out his reasoning to me carefully. He said that the woman's agitation, the secrecy, the sum of money, the proximity of the cottage to the Monroe household—all pointed in a particular direction. He even sent Mr. Monroe home with a set of instructions: to report back if anything further came to light, and above all not to take any impulsive action himself.

**SMITH**: And impulsive action, Mr. Monroe, was precisely what you took.

**GRANT MONROE**: I am afraid it was. I will not pretend otherwise. Holmes had told me to wait, and I tried. But on a particular evening I could endure the uncertainty no longer. I saw the light in the cottage window from my own house. I knew Effie was in there. I went across, and I went in.

**WATSON**: Holmes and I had also made our way to Norbury that same evening, as it happens. Mr. Monroe's situation had continued to weigh on Holmes, and he wished to observe the neighborhood at closer hand. We arrived just as things were reaching their conclusion.

**SMITH**: Mr. Monroe, tell us, if you will, what you found when you entered that cottage.

**GRANT MONROE**: I found Effie. And with her was a small child—a little girl. The child's face was covered by a mask, a yellowish thing that I had seen at the window on the earlier occasion. When I entered, Effie pulled the mask away from the child's face. And I saw—I saw that the child's complexion was dark. Darker than Effie's, darker than my own. I understood in that moment the connection to Effie's first husband, Mr. Hebron, and I understood why Effie had been so afraid to tell me.

**SMITH**: That was a moment that required a great deal of you, Mr. Monroe.

**GRANT MONROE**: It did. But I hope—I believe—that I did not fail it. I asked Effie the child's name. She told me it was Lucy. I took Lucy in my arms.

**EFFIE MONROE**: That is what he did. He took her in his arms, and he held her. I had been so afraid, and in that moment all of my fear simply vanished.

**SMITH**: Miss Lucy, you were very young at the time of these events. Do you have any memory of that evening, or of the period in the cottage?

**LUCY MONROE**: I remember the cottage. I remember the lady who was with me there. And I remember the mask. I did not like wearing it. It was uncomfortable, and I did not fully understand why I had to. I remember the evening my mother came with my—with my father. He was tall, and he lifted me, and I remember that very well.

**EFFIE MONROE**: I had explained to Lucy that she was to wear the mask when she went near the window, and when strangers came. I wanted to protect her from curious eyes. I realize now that it was the mask itself that had drawn attention, rather than deflected it. It was one of several errors of judgment I made during that period.

**SMITH**: Mrs. Monroe, I want to press a little on the question of why you kept this secret. You have said that you were afraid. But you knew your husband to be a man of good character. What precisely did you fear?

**EFFIE MONROE**: I feared—I feared many things. I feared that his feelings for me might change, that knowing I had a child by a previous marriage, and a child whose appearance was as it is, might alter how he saw me, or how he saw our life together. I feared that society's opinion would be a burden he had not contracted for when he married me. These may not be rational fears, and looking back, I know they were unfair to Grant. He is a better man than my fears gave him credit for. But fear is not always rational.

**GRANT MONROE**: I have told Effie since that I wish she had trusted me sooner. But I also understand why she did not. People are not always what they should be in such circumstances, and she had no certainty of how I would react. I choose not to dwell on the months of estrangement that her silence caused between us. We are past it.

**SMITH**: Dr. Watson, let us now address what is, I think, the rather remarkable feature of this case from the perspective of our regular seminars. Holmes, as you have noted, formed a theory. That theory was wrong. This is, I believe, among the very few cases you have recorded in which Holmes was quite so thoroughly mistaken in his conclusions. How did he receive that knowledge?

**WATSON**: I have to say—and I trust Holmes will forgive my saying so, though he is not with us today—that it was an instructive moment. When Grant Monroe emerged from the cottage with the child in his arms, and when the true nature of the situation became plain, Holmes stood very quietly for a little while. He was not a man who wore embarrassment openly, but there was a quality to his silence that told me a great deal.

**DOYLE**: Watson's notes include a passage I found particularly striking when he sent them to me. He records that Holmes went to where Watson and Monroe were standing and said—and these are Watson's words—that if he ever seemed to become a little over-confident in his own powers, or gave the impression of being too certain of the outcome of a case, Watson was to whisper the word "Norbury" to him. I thought that quite remarkable.

**WATSON**: I found it remarkable too. It was, I think, a genuine expression of something Holmes felt strongly in that moment. He had reasoned himself into a confident position, and the facts had not supported it. He was not a man who took such things lightly. I have used the word once or twice since, on occasions when I thought it might be warranted.

**SMITH**: And the effect?

**WATSON**: Let us simply say it has never failed to produce a brief but noticeable pause for reflection.

**SMITH**: Mr. Monroe, I wonder if you have any view on Holmes's role in the affair. He did not, in the event, solve the case in the conventional sense. The truth came out through your own actions, not through his deductions.

**GRANT MONROE**: That is so. And yet I would not say that Holmes was without value in the matter. Speaking with him—laying out everything I knew, being obliged to organize my own thoughts clearly enough to present them—was useful to me. And Holmes was quite correct on one essential point: he counseled me not to act impulsively, not to confront Effie or enter the cottage without more information. I did not follow that counsel, and although it turned out well, it might very easily have gone otherwise.

**EFFIE MONROE**: I am glad it went as it did. But Grant arrived at the cottage in a state of some agitation, and had he arrived in that state to find something other than what he found, I think the outcome might have been quite different. Holmes's instinct to proceed carefully was sound, even if his theory was not.

**SMITH**: Arthur, as the person who shaped these events into narrative form for the public, what drew you to include this particular case? It is not, after all, a case that reflects especially well upon Holmes.

**DOYLE**: No, it is not. And that is precisely why I included it. I have always been of the view that Holmes is best rendered honestly—as a man of extraordinary gifts, certainly, but a man nonetheless, and therefore fallible. A story in which Holmes is always right, in which his powers are never shown to have limits, would ultimately be less interesting, and less truthful, than one which admits of the occasional error. The Yellow Face is that admission. And it seemed to me that the emotional heart of the case—the reunion of Effie and Lucy, and Grant Monroe's response to it—was of greater human significance than any feat of deduction could have been. It is, in some respects, the most quietly moving of all the cases Watson has furnished to me.

**WATSON**: I would not argue with that. When I wrote up my notes, I was struck by how the real resolution of the case had nothing to do with Holmes's method. It came from a husband's character, and from a mother's love. Holmes observed afterwards that Watson had done a better job of capturing the human element than he himself had done of capturing the truth, and that struck me as a very gracious thing for him to say.

**SMITH**: Miss Lucy, you are now old enough to understand something of how the world has received this story, which was published by The Strand. Does it feel strange to you, knowing that your own story—the story of the yellow face at the window, the cottage, the mask—has been read by so many people?

**LUCY MONROE**: It does feel strange, yes. I did not ask for it, and I did not know for some time that it had been written at all. But my mother and father explained it to me carefully, and they told me that if anyone treated me differently because of it, that was a fault in them and not in me. I think Mr. Doyle told the truth in it, and I think the truth is worth telling.

**EFFIE MONROE**: Lucy is not wrong. We have received letters—a number of them—from people who read the story and were moved by it. Some of those letters came from people whose own lives were touched by circumstances not entirely unlike ours. I have kept one or two of them.

**SMITH**: That is a remarkable testimony to the power of the story. Arthur, Dr. Watson, I think we must be approaching our final quarter-hour. Are there observations you would like to add before we open the floor?

**DOYLE**: Only this: the case of the Yellow Face is, among other things, a story about what happens when secrecy, however well-intentioned, corrodes the trust upon which a marriage depends. Effie's motives were not selfish ones. She acted out of fear and out of love for her daughter. But the withholding of truth has consequences, and for a time those consequences weighed very heavily on the Monroe household. I think that is a lesson that resonates well beyond any particular set of circumstances.

**WATSON**: And the case is also, I think, a reminder that Mr. Holmes, for all his gifts, was always most useful in cases that had a logical solution. The Yellow Face was a human problem, not a logical one. It was solved by a man choosing well in a difficult moment. Holmes could have analyzed the situation for a fortnight and not produced a better outcome than Grant Monroe produced by walking through that cottage door with an open heart.

**GRANT MONROE**: I am grateful for Dr. Watson's generous reading of my actions. I am not sure I deserve quite so charitable a description. I went through that door in a state bordering on desperation. If it turned out to be the right thing to do, a great deal of that was owing to luck.

**EFFIE MONROE**: It was not luck, Grant. I have told you that before.

**GRANT MONROE**: My wife is more generous to me than I am to myself. Perhaps that is as it should be.

**SMITH**: On that note, I think we have a question from our audience.

*Note: The audience questions which followed have not been transcribed in full. Highlights are recorded below*

**AUDIENCE MEMBER** [unidentified]: Mrs. Monroe, were you ever afraid that Mr. Holmes would discover the truth before you were ready to reveal it yourself?

**EFFIE MONROE**: Every day that he was engaged on the matter, yes. I knew, from what Grant had told me of him, that he was a man of remarkable penetration. I feared he would find his way to Lucy before I could find my courage. As it turned out, he reached a different conclusion entirely. I confess there was a moment—quite an unworthy moment—when I felt something close to relief that he had been mistaken.

**AUDIENCE MEMBER** [unidentified]: Dr. Watson, do you believe Holmes learned from this case?

**WATSON**: I believe he did. I would not say that it changed his method—his method was his method, and I have never known him to abandon it. But I think it introduced, or perhaps reinforced, a note of humility that was not always present in the early years of my acquaintance with him. He became somewhat more careful, after Norbury, about the point at which he committed himself publicly to a conclusion. Somewhat more careful. He was not, by nature, a diffident man.

**SMITH**: We have time for one final observation from the panel, if any of you would care to offer it. Mr. Monroe, shall we give you the last word?

**GRANT MONROE**: Very well. I shall say only this: when I walked into that cottage, I did not know what I would find, and I did not know what kind of man I would prove to be when I found it. We none of us know that, until the moment comes. I am glad—more glad than I can easily say—that when the moment came, I did not disgrace myself or the people I love. Everything good that has come to our family since that evening has its foundation in what happened in that room. I am grateful for it every day.

**SMITH**: Truer words were never spoken. Well, our has come to say goodbye. On behalf of The Strand Magazine and the British Museum, I bid you all farewell.

*Sustained applause*

# The Stockbroker's Clerk

*First Published in March, 1893*
*Sponsored by The Strand Magazine*
*Meeting Room B, British Museum, London*

**The Eighteenth Seminar**

**Herbert Greenhough Smith** — The Strand Editor & Moderator
**Arthur Conan Doyle** — Author and Watson's Literary Agent
**Dr. John H. Watson** —Colleague and Biographer of Sherlock Holmes
**Mr. Hall Pycroft** — Client of Mr. Sherlock Holmes & Stockbroker
**Sergeant Tuson** — City Policeman who helped catch elder Beddington
**Constable Pollock** — Assisted Sergeant Tuson with capture

Seminar Transcript

**SMITH**: Good evening, ladies and gentlemen, and welcome to the eighteenth in our series of seminars commemorating the remarkable adventures of Mr. Sherlock Holmes, as published here in the pages of the Strand Magazine. We are, as always, convened in the splendid hospitality of this public meeting room at the British Museum. Tonight's story is one which took our principals not only through the streets of London but also to the great industrial city of Birmingham — and which turned upon the twin forces of ambition and deceit. The story in question is, of course, "The Stockbroker's Clerk." I am joined, as ever, by Arthur Conan Doyle, who gave this tale its literary form, and by Dr. John H. Watson, who furnished Arthur with the notes upon which the account was based. We are also very pleased to welcome tonight three gentlemen who played direct parts in the matter: Mr. Hall Pycroft, the young clerk who found himself at the centre of the affair; Sergeant Tuson of the Metropolitan Police; and Constable Pollock, also of the Metropolitan Police. Gentlemen, you are all most heartily welcome.

*Murmurs of appreciation from the audience*

**SMITH:** Dr. Watson, let us begin, as we usually do, with you. Will you set the scene for our audience this evening?

**WATSON:** With pleasure, Smith. The events you are about to hear discussed took place when I had settled into a practice in the Paddington district. Holmes was still at Baker Street, and I had fallen somewhat out of the habit of dropping in upon him as regularly as I once had. One morning, however, he paid a call on me — quite unexpectedly, I should say — and it was not long before we were both of us drawn into what proved to be a very remarkable business. Mr. Pycroft here was the man who brought it before us, though he did not come to us directly at first. Holmes and I, in fact, travelled to Birmingham to seek him out.

**SMITH:** Indeed. Arthur, the story as it appeared in the Strand presented the affair rather compactly. Were there elements that struck you, in the notes Dr. Watson provided, as particularly unusual?

**DOYLE:** There were several, Mr. Smith. What struck me most forcibly was the sheer audacity of the scheme at the heart of it — the idea that a man might be deliberately maneuvered out of a position he had legitimately secured, kept busy with a meaningless occupation in another city, all so that a criminal impersonator might step into his shoes. It is a plot of considerable ingenuity, and I confess that when Watson first laid the notes before me, I had to read through them twice before I fully appreciated the elegance — and the wickedness — of the design. It was the sort of scheme that could only have been devised by someone with a thorough knowledge of how the great financial houses conducted their business.

**SMITH:** And that financial house, of course, was Mawson and Williams. Mr. Pycroft, let us turn to you. Will you tell us, in your own words, how this whole affair first began for you?

**PYCROFT:** Gladly, Mr. Smith, though I confess the memory still unsettles me somewhat. I had been out of work for some weeks, as I think is known, and I had at last secured a position — a very good position, as I believed — at Mawson and Williams. I was to start there on a Monday, and I was, naturally, in excellent spirits. Then, on the very Saturday before I was to begin, a man came to call upon me at my lodgings in the Avenue, Tottenham Court Road. He introduced himself as Mr. Arthur Pinner, of the Franco-Midland Hardware Company, Limited. He was a dark fellow, well dressed, with a full beard and a glittering gold tooth that showed whenever he smiled, which was often enough.

**SMITH:** And what did this Mr. Pinner want with you?

**PYCROFT:** He wanted to offer me a position, Mr. Smith. Not a clerkship, mind you, but a managerial appointment — the position of business manager for the whole of the Franco-Midland Hardware Company's operations, with a salary of five hundred pounds per year. I had never earned anything approaching such a sum. The firm, he explained, had one hundred and thirty-four branches across the Continent and was expanding into England and Wales. He had been making enquiries about suitable men and had heard of me through someone who knew my work.

**SMITH:** And naturally that offer was attractive to you.

**PYCROFT:** Attractive! Mr. Smith, I was nearly beside myself. Here I had been scrabbling about looking for ordinary clerk's work, and here was a man offering me five hundred a year. Of course, there was one condition — I was to give up the Mawson and Williams position entirely, before I had even begun it. Mr. Pinner said that his company needed me at once and could not have me compromising their interests by maintaining a connection with a rival firm in the City.

**SMITH:** Dr. Watson, I believe there came a point where Mr. Holmes had occasion to examine the letter Mr. Pycroft had received from Mr. Pinner. Did Holmes remark upon anything?

**WATSON:** He did, yes. He noted, with his characteristic precision, certain peculiarities — and the absence of the company's name on the prospectus, which Pycroft was given, struck him as odd. But more than that, what puzzled Holmes greatly was the reason offered for Pycroft being given a hundred pounds in advance of his employment — banknotes, as I recall.

**PYCROFT:** That is correct. Pinner said it was the custom of the company to make an advance of that kind to its managers. I did think it generous at the time, though in hindsight it was simply a means of ensuring my compliance and of keeping me from wondering too hard about the arrangement.

**SMITH:** Arthur, from a narrative standpoint, the advance of the hundred pounds serves a rather clever double function, does it not?

**DOYLE:** Precisely so. On the one hand, it binds Pycroft — he has accepted money, he has given up his position at Mawson and Williams, and he is therefore committed. On the other hand, it establishes, in the reader's mind — and, one might say, in the mind of the investigators — that whoever was behind the scheme was not short of funds. This was not a petty swindle. There was capital behind it, and therefore a larger crime somewhere waiting to be uncovered.

**SMITH:** Mr. Pycroft, will you tell us what happened when you went to Birmingham?

**PYCROFT:** I arrived in Birmingham as arranged and presented myself at the Corporation Street address I had been given. There I met another man who introduced himself as Mr. Harry Pinner, the brother of Arthur Pinner who had come to see me in London. Now, Harry Pinner was very like his brother in many respects — similar complexion, similar build — but what caught my eye, and what I could not get out of my head as the days went on, was that Harry Pinner also had a gold tooth, in precisely the same position in his mouth as Arthur Pinner's.

**SMITH:** And you found that remarkable.

**PYCROFT:** I did, though I confess I could not have told you at the time exactly why it troubled me. The two men seemed very different in manner — Arthur had been confident and smooth in London, whereas Harry in Birmingham was more agitated, more watchful. But there was something in the way each of them wore that same gold tooth that nagged at me.

**WATSON:** It was, in fact, Holmes who seized upon that detail immediately when Pycroft described it to us. I remember he sat up very straight and said something to the effect that it was the most remarkable thing he had heard, that two brothers should each have a tooth capped in gold in the same position. I did not follow his reasoning at first.

**SMITH:** Arthur, what was the significance, as Holmes understood it?

**DOYLE:** Simply this — that it was almost certainly not two brothers at all, but the same man. The same individual had been in London posing as Arthur Pinner and in Birmingham posing as Harry Pinner. The gold tooth, far from being a coincidence to be wondered at, was actually the identifying mark that revealed the imposture. It takes a man of Holmes's observational powers to treat a seemingly innocent physical detail as the decisive clue.

**SMITH:** Mr. Pycroft, what work were you actually set to doing in Birmingham?

**PYCROFT:** That is where the absurdity of it becomes plain, looking back. I was given a copy of a trade directory — a large volume — and was set to copying out names from it into a notebook. Names of hardware dealers, I believe, or some such category. I was told this was essential preparatory work for the company's expansion into England. I sat at a desk for hours doing this. It was dull beyond description, but I was being paid generously and I assumed it was simply the sort of drudgery that attended the early stages of a new enterprise.

**SMITH:** Holmes's view of that assignment was rather different, I take it?

**WATSON:** Holmes saw through it in an instant. When Pycroft described the work to us, Holmes said that it was perfectly plain that the whole business was simply a device to keep Pycroft occupied and out of London. The task had no genuine commercial value. It was, in essence, busy-work — designed to prevent Pycroft from appearing at Mawson and Williams on that Monday morning, so that someone else could take his place.

**SMITH:** And who, precisely, was that someone else?

**DOYLE:** The man who had posed as Arthur Pinner in London — the same man who had been posing as Harry Pinner in Birmingham. He and his confederate were, in truth, the Beddington brothers, well-known criminals who had been involved in a forgery case some years earlier. One of them took Pycroft's identity and used the references Pycroft had furnished to secure himself a place at Mawson and Williams — in Pycroft's name — with the intention of robbing the firm of a very considerable sum in securities.

**SMITH:** How considerable a sum?

**WATSON:** The newspaper report that came into our hands that morning, just as Holmes and Pycroft and I were at the offices in Birmingham, mentioned fifty thousand pounds worth of negotiable securities. It was a robbery of the first magnitude.

*Audible gasps from the audience*

**SMITH:** Fifty thousand pounds. Quite extraordinary. Now, gentlemen, I think we must now bring Sergeant Tuson and Constable Pollock into our conversation, for it was they who arrived upon the scene at what proved to be a very dramatic moment. Sergeant Tuson, will you describe the circumstances of your attendance?

**TUSON:** Certainly, Mr. Smith. Constable Pollock and I received word that there had been an incident at premises in Corporation Street — the offices of what was represented to us as the Franco-Midland Hardware Company. We attended without delay. When we arrived, we found three gentlemen already on the scene, one of whom identified himself to me as Mr. Sherlock Holmes — a name I knew, of course — another as Dr. Watson, and the third as Mr. Pycroft here. The reason we had been sent for was that a man had been found hanging.

**SMITH:** Hanging? Will you describe what you found?

**TUSON:** The man had suspended himself from a hook behind the office door, using his own cravat as the means. He had not succeeded in completing the act, however. Holmes and his companions had cut him down before we arrived, and the man was alive, though insensible. It was, I will say, a very grim sight, even for those of us accustomed to such things. There was no mistaking what had been intended.

**SMITH:** Constable Pollock, you were present as well. What were your impressions on arriving?

**POLLOCK:** I was struck first by the state of the room, Mr. Smith. It was not a particularly well-appointed office to begin with, but there was evidence of considerable agitation — a newspaper lying open on the desk, as I recall. It was made clear to me fairly quickly that the cause of the man's distress was something he had read in that newspaper. The arrest of his confederate in London, as I understood it afterward, was what had driven him to the act.

**SMITH:** Dr. Watson, can you tell us how it was that Holmes and you came to be present in that office at precisely the moment this occurred?

**WATSON:** We had gone to the office that morning together with Pycroft, at Holmes's instigation. Holmes had, by that point, worked out the substance of the scheme, and he wished to confront Harry Pinner — or rather, the man calling himself Harry Pinner — directly. He had observed that Pycroft's employment was a fabrication, he had identified the likely purpose of keeping Pycroft from Mawson and Williams, and he believed that matters were coming to a head. We entered the office and found the man there. Holmes put certain questions to him — rather pointed ones. Then Pycroft, following Holmes's lead, produced the newspaper, which contained the report of the arrest at Mawson and Williams. The effect upon the man was instantaneous and dreadful. He rushed from the room before any of us could stop him, and when we followed within moments, we found him as Sergeant Tuson has described.

**SMITH:** Mr. Pycroft, that must have been a most alarming spectacle.

**PYCROFT:** Alarming is rather too mild a word for it, Mr. Smith. I had spent several weeks working for this man, talking with him daily, taking his money. And yet he had meant to use me all along as nothing more than a tool in a criminal enterprise. When I saw him lying there on the floor, cut down from that hook, I confess my feelings were rather mixed. Anger, certainly. But also, I am not ashamed to say, something approaching pity. He had gone to very great lengths, and the whole scheme had collapsed about him in an instant, with a single newspaper report.

**SMITH:** Sergeant Tuson, what were the formalities that followed? How did you proceed once you had attended to the immediate crisis?

**TUSON:** The man was conveyed for medical attention. That was the immediate priority, as he was still living. Constable Pollock took down the particulars from those present — Mr. Holmes, Dr. Watson, and Mr. Pycroft — so that there would be a proper record. Mr. Holmes was most helpful in that regard; he was precise and thorough in the account he gave, which made our work considerably easier. We had also, of course, to liaise with our colleagues in London, where the more serious charge arising from the robbery at Mawson and Williams was already being dealt with.

**POLLOCK:** I will add, if I may, that Mr. Holmes made a particular point of ensuring that Mr. Pycroft's own position was clearly established from the outset — that he had had no knowledge of, and had played no willing part in, the conspiracy. That was important for Mr. Pycroft's sake.

**PYCROFT:** And I am very grateful for it, Constable, as I was at the time. It is a peculiar position to be in — to have had your name and references used by a criminal, without your knowledge or consent, in the furtherance of a crime. I was concerned that there might be questions about my own conduct, and Mr. Holmes's clarity on that point was a very great relief to me.

**SMITH:** Arthur, the story ends rather briskly, as so many of the Holmes tales do. The legal outcome is dispensed with in a sentence or two. Was that Watson's own economy in the notes, or a choice you made in the writing?

**DOYLE:** A little of both, I think. Watson's notes are always admirably focused on the investigation itself — on what Holmes said and did, and on the human drama of the individuals involved. The legal proceedings that follow are, from a narrative standpoint, a denouement rather than a climax. The climax is the discovery, the unmasking. Once that has occurred, the reader is satisfied, and to extend the story further into courtroom proceedings and sentences would, I think, dissipate the tension that has been built up. Holmes himself, I suspect, would agree — once the intellectual problem is solved, the rest is merely administration.

**WATSON:** Holmes did once remark to me — though not in connection with this case specifically — that the work of the detective ends when the truth is established. What the law subsequently does with that truth is a separate matter entirely.

**SMITH:** Dr. Watson, I should like to ask you about Holmes himself in this case. We know he had been unwell for some time — he mentions it in connection with this story. How did he seem to you when he called upon you?

**WATSON:** He had indeed been ill, and it showed. He was thinner than I remembered, and there was something about his manner — a restless energy, a keenness — that suggested he had been chafing at inactivity. As a medical man, I was not entirely satisfied with his condition. But when he described the matter that had been brought to his attention, and explained why he wished me to accompany him to Birmingham, all such considerations fell away. Holmes in pursuit of a case is altogether a different proposition from Holmes at rest.

**SMITH:** Mr. Pycroft, with the benefit of hindsight, were there any moments during your weeks in Birmingham when you ought, perhaps, to have been more suspicious?

**PYCROFT:** Oh, a great many, Mr. Smith. The work I was given was conspicuously without purpose. Any clerk with half a brain ought to have asked why the manager of a hardware company was being asked to copy names from a directory rather than actually managing anything. And Harry Pinner — the man who called himself that — was plainly in a state of nerves much of the time. He watched me very carefully, asked after my health and whether I intended to remain in Birmingham, inquired whether I had written to anyone in London. At the time I attributed it to the eccentricities of a new employer. Looking back, every one of those enquiries was a measure of how anxious he was that I should not discover what was happening in London under my name.

**SMITH:** Sergeant Tuson, in your experience, is the kind of scheme employed here — the substitution of one man's identity for another's — a common device among criminals of this sort?

**TUSON:** It is not unknown, Mr. Smith, particularly in cases involving financial houses and establishments where a new employee's references and history are the chief means of assessing their trustworthiness. A man who can secure genuine references, or who can obtain them by deception, gains a degree of credibility that is very difficult for the firm to see through in ordinary circumstances. What made this case somewhat unusual was the elaborateness of the arrangements made to keep the real Mr. Pycroft entirely out of the way. Most such schemes rely on the victim's ignorance alone. This one went a step further and actively managed him.

**SMITH:** Constable Pollock, you are the youngest of our guests this evening. Was this case, if you will forgive my asking, your first encounter with Mr. Holmes or Dr. Watson?

**POLLOCK:** It was, Mr. Smith. I had heard of Mr. Holmes, naturally — everyone in the force had. But I had not previously had occasion to meet him. I will confess that when I arrived at that office and was told that the tall, lean gentleman standing in the corner was Sherlock Holmes, I looked at him rather more carefully than I might otherwise have done. He struck me as a man who was in the habit of observing everyone else while giving away very little of himself in return.

**WATSON:** That is an excellent description of him, Constable. I have known Holmes for many years and I would say it is precisely accurate.

*Laughter from the audience and the panel*

**SMITH:** Dr. Watson, one more question before we open the floor. It has been remarked by several of our audiences in previous seminars that Holmes's methods seem, on occasion, almost theatrical — that he enjoys the unmasking, the moment of revelation. Did you see that quality in him during this case?

**WATSON:** I did, yes. When Holmes began his questioning of the man who called himself Harry Pinner that morning, there was a deliberateness about it — a patience in the way he laid his questions — that made me aware he was not simply gathering information. He already had the information. He was constructing something, building toward a point. And when Pycroft produced the newspaper and placed it on the desk, I saw in Holmes's face something that I can only describe as quiet satisfaction — the satisfaction of a man who has placed the final piece of a design exactly where it belongs.

**PYCROFT:** I can confirm that, Dr. Watson. I was watching Holmes almost as closely as I was watching Pinner. And I remember thinking, even in the midst of all that confusion and alarm, that this was a man who was entirely in command of the situation — who had known, before any of us did, exactly how the scene was going to play out.

**SMITH:** Gentlemen, it remains only for me to thank you all. Mr. Pycroft, you have been most candid about what must have been a deeply unsettling episode in your life, and we are grateful for your frankness. Sergeant Tuson and Constable Pollock, the police in these stories are sometimes treated by the readership as foils to Mr. Holmes's genius, and it is a great pleasure to hear from officers who attended the scene and to be reminded that it is their quiet professionalism that ensures the machinery of justice is set in motion once the detection is done. Dr. Watson, your notes gave Arthur the raw material, and the account you have provided us this evening has filled in the texture of events most admirably. And Arthur, your telling of this tale in the pages of the Strand is, as always, a model of the form.

*Applause from the audience*

**DOYLE:** Thank you, Smith. I would add only this — that of all the elements in "The Stockbroker's Clerk" that I found compelling as a writer, it is the figure of Hall Pycroft that I return to most often in my thoughts. He is not a client in any conventional sense — he had not even sought Holmes out. He is, rather, a young man of decent ability and genuine ambition who was identified precisely because of those qualities and exploited accordingly. There is something rather poignant in that, I think. And something rather admirable in the equanimity with which he has discussed it this evening.

**PYCROFT:** You are very kind, Arthur. I will say only that if any good came of the whole affair, it was this: I have since learned to be rather more careful when a stranger appears at my door offering five hundred pounds a year.

*Warm laughter from the audience*

**SMITH:** On that note, ladies and gentlemen, we bring Seminar the Eighteenth to a close. Good evening to you all.

*Prolonged applause as participants rise and take their leave of the stage*

# The Gloria Scott

*First Published in April, 1893*
*Sponsored by The Strand Magazine*
*Meeting Room B, British Museum, London*

## The Nineteenth Seminar

**Herbert Greenhough Smith** — The Strand Editor & Moderator
**Arthur Conan Doyle** — Author and Watson's Literary Agent
**Dr. John H. Watson** —Colleague and Biographer of Sherlock Holmes
**Mr. Victor Trevor** — Friend of Sherlock Holmes from College

Seminar Transcript

**SMITH:** Good afternoon, ladies and gentlemen, and welcome to the nineteenth in our series of commemorative seminars devoted to the recorded investigations of Mr. Sherlock Holmes. I am Herbert Greenhough Smith, editor of The Strand Magazine, and I am once again privileged to serve as your moderator. Joining me today, as always, is Arthur Conan Doyle, who has brought these remarkable cases to the reading public, and Dr. John H. Watson, whose meticulous case notes have provided the foundation for every story we have thus far discussed. We are additionally honored this afternoon by the presence of Mr. Victor Trevor, whose personal connection to today's story is both singular and profound. Gentlemen, welcome, and thank you all for being here.

**DOYLE:** Thank you, Smith. It is always a pleasure to be in this room, and I confess that today's story occupies a rather special place in my regard for the entire canon, as it were. There is something distinctly moving about a tale that takes us back to the very origins of Holmes's career as a consulting detective.

**WATSON:** I should say at the outset that my own role in this particular narrative is, for once, largely that of a listener rather than a participant. Holmes himself was good enough to share the story with me one winter evening, when we were sitting together at Baker Street and he was moved to speak of it. The case predates my acquaintance with him by some years, and therefore the notes I furnished to Doyle were drawn from my own transcription of Holmes's account, supplemented by the remarkable written document which Mr. Trevor was kind enough to allow Holmes to retain.

**TREVOR:** I am glad to be here, though I will admit, gentlemen, that revisiting these events is not without a certain weight. My father's memory is not a simple thing to speak of in a public setting. But I have come to believe, in the years since, that the story deserves to be told fully and honestly, and if this occasion serves that purpose, then I am content to participate in it.

**SMITH:** We are grateful for your candor, Mr. Trevor, and we shall proceed with all appropriate care for the sensitivities involved. Let us begin, as Holmes himself began when he told the tale to Dr. Watson, at the university. Arthur, would you set the scene for our audience?

**DOYLE:** Gladly. The story opens with Holmes himself furnishing Watson with an account of his earliest case — a case which he describes as the one which first gave him some indication that he possessed talent that might be turned to practical account. Holmes and Victor Trevor were, at the time, both students at university, and Holmes, who had few close acquaintances there, counted Victor Trevor as, in his own words, his only friend. He describes himself as unsociable and finding his nature out of touch with his fellow students, so the friendship was a notable exception.

**WATSON:** Holmes was, even then, already applying himself to observation and deduction as a kind of private exercise. He has told me that he was not yet thinking of it as a profession; it was more in the nature of a habit of mind, a method by which he engaged with the world. But the friendship with Mr. Trevor gave that habit its first real test.

**SMITH:** Mr. Trevor, how did your acquaintance with Holmes begin? It is my understanding that there was a rather violent commencement to the friendship.

**TREVOR:** Violent is not too strong a word, Mr. Smith. My father kept a bull terrier, a fine animal but one of unpredictable temper. Holmes had some occasion to pass near it, and the dog seized him by the ankle. The injury was not catastrophic, but it laid Holmes up for some ten days, and during that period I called upon him regularly to see how he was getting on. That is how we became friends. One might say the dog did us both a service, though I doubt either Holmes or the ankle would agree with that assessment.

**DOYLE:** It is a wonderfully ironic beginning. Holmes, who would later become famous for drawing the most far-reaching conclusions from the smallest of observations, was brought low by the most straightforward of mishaps — a dog and an ankle.

**WATSON:** Holmes himself told the story with a wry amusement. He bore no grudge against the animal, as I recall him saying.

**SMITH:** And it was shortly after this friendship was established that Holmes paid his first visit to your father's estate, was it not, Mr. Trevor? At Donnithorpe, in Norfolk?

**TREVOR:** That is correct. My father's home was at Donnithorpe, and I had pressed Holmes to come and stay with us for a month in the summer. He agreed, and it was during that visit that he first encountered my father, Mr. James Trevor — as we then knew him — and exercised upon him those faculties of observation for which he has since become so celebrated.

**SMITH:** Doyle, perhaps you could describe those observations for our audience, as Holmes recorded them?

**DOYLE:** With pleasure. When Holmes first met the elder Mr. Trevor, he drew from a careful examination of the man a series of conclusions that rather astonished their subject. He observed, from a tattoo on his arm, that the initials "J.A." had at some point been worked there and subsequently obscured, though not entirely. He noted from various physical signs that Mr. Trevor had known hard physical labor in his earlier years, and had spent time in the tropics. He made certain deductions concerning the man's health and prior anxieties. And — most crucially as it turned out — he referred to the initials on the tattoo in some manner that caused the older man to turn white and collapse very nearly in a faint.

**TREVOR:** I was present when it happened. I had never seen my father discomposed in that way. He was, as a general rule, a composed and self-possessed man — a justice of the peace, respected in the county, a man who carried himself with the quiet authority of someone whose affairs were in order. But when Holmes spoke those few words about the tattoo, something happened in my father's face that I had never seen there before. It was as though a figure from another world had suddenly stepped into the room.

**WATSON:** Holmes described to me afterwards his own reaction to that moment. He said he had not yet understood the significance of what he had observed — only that the reaction of the elder Mr. Trevor was entirely disproportionate to what had been said, and that disproportionate reactions are, in his view, among the most reliable indicators that something of importance lies beneath the surface.

**SMITH:** And yet, despite this alarming episode, your father recovered himself and the visit continued pleasantly, as I understand it?

**TREVOR:** It did. My father spoke to Holmes privately the following morning and expressed his admiration for Holmes's gifts, and the three of us got on extremely well for the remainder of the stay. Holmes has a quality, which I think Watson will recognize, of being able to set a person at their ease once the moment of initial shock has passed. He did not press my father on the matter of the tattoo, and my father did not raise it again, and we all behaved as though nothing of consequence had occurred.

**WATSON:** That restraint is characteristic of Holmes at his best. He knows that information volunteered freely is generally more complete and more reliable than information extracted by pressure.

**SMITH:** The visit, however, was not to end without further disturbance. There was the matter of a visitor — a man named Hudson.

**TREVOR:** Yes. Hudson. I can speak of him now with a degree of composure I would not have possessed at the time. He arrived at Donnithorpe without invitation, a rough, weathered man of seafaring appearance, coarse in his manner and entirely familiar with my father in a way that was wholly inappropriate to any legitimate relationship between them. And my father received him — that is the word I must use, received him — with a deference that was nothing short of shocking to me.

**DOYLE:** Holmes recorded his impressions of Hudson with characteristic precision. He describes him as a small, dark, wizened man, with a face that was deeply lined and a manner that combined a certain servility of surface with something that he sensed was profoundly threatening underneath.

**WATSON:** Holmes told me that it was the contrast between the elder Mr. Trevor's obvious standing in the community and the latitude he extended to this man Hudson that struck him as the most telling feature of the situation. A man of your father's position, Mr. Trevor, did not ordinarily tolerate that sort of familiarity from a social inferior without very compelling reason.

**TREVOR:** Holmes is perfectly correct. My father was not a weak or timid man in any ordinary sense. He was decisive and rather domineering, in fact, when it came to the management of his estate and his household. To see him practically cringe before Hudson — and that is the honest word for it, cringe — was a revelation that I did not at the time know how to interpret.

**SMITH:** Holmes, in his account, was not insensible to the peculiarity of the situation, but he had no basis at that point for understanding its source. He departed from Donnithorpe at the end of the visit without, as I understand it, any clear resolution to the mystery.

**DOYLE:** That is correct. He left with his observations and his unease, but without any key to the cipher. That key came later, and from a terrible direction.

**SMITH:** Let us speak of that, then. Mr. Trevor, perhaps you can describe what happened in the weeks following Holmes's departure.

**TREVOR:** Hudson remained at Donnithorpe, and his behavior grew steadily worse. He had, it became clear, some hold over my father that gave him an effective immunity from any normal consequences of his conduct. He was insolent to the household staff, he drank heavily, and he treated the establishment as though it were his own. My father endured all of this with a patience that I can only now understand was born of desperation rather than indulgence.

**WATSON:** Holmes, when he received word of what was happening, observed that Hudson appeared to be exploiting his position to its fullest extent, and that the nature of the hold must be both powerful and old to have produced such complete submission.

**TREVOR:** Eventually my father arranged for Hudson to go to a man named Beddoes, who lived in Hampshire. Beddoes was, as I learned later, another survivor of the same catastrophe that had shaped my father's life. The arrangement appeared to relieve my father for a time. But then came the letter.

**SMITH:** Ah. The cipher letter. Doyle, I think this is one of the most ingenious features of the entire story, and I suspect our audience would be grateful if you explained it in some detail.

**DOYLE:** It is a marvelous piece of construction. A letter arrived for the elder Mr. Trevor which, on its surface, appeared to be nothing more than a note about game supplies and the affairs of a head-keeper named Hudson. The surface meaning was entirely mundane. But Holmes, examining it after the catastrophe it caused, recognized at once that it was a cipher, and that the method of encryption was straightforward once you had the key: you read every third word. When he applied that method, the message read: 'The game is up. Hudson has told all. Fly for your life.'

**WATSON:** Holmes described to me the elegance of the thing — not merely as a cryptographic exercise, but as a glimpse into the psychology of men who had long ago learned to communicate in secret. The letter was the product of a world my father's generation had largely buried, and it had the quality of an old debt suddenly called in.

**TREVOR:** My father read that letter. I do not know whether he worked out the cipher himself or whether the plain text of it struck him by some other means. I found him in his study, the letter on the floor beside him. He had suffered a severe fit. He lingered for some days, but he never recovered, and he died without regaining the clarity of mind that might have allowed him to explain himself.

**SMITH:** I am very sorry, Mr. Trevor. It is a profound tragedy.

**TREVOR:** It was. And the cruelty of it is that my father was, by the time of his death, a genuinely good man. Whatever he had done in his youth, whatever desperation or weakness had led him to the actions that gave Hudson his hold, the man I knew was a fair landlord, a respected magistrate, and a devoted father. He had built a good life honestly and had tried to leave the past where it lay.

**DOYLE:** That tension is, I think, one of the most morally complex elements of the story. The case raises, in a very direct way, the question of how far a man's early transgressions should pursue him through the whole of a reformed life.

**WATSON:** Holmes did not, as I recall, offer any pronounced moral verdict on the elder Mr. Trevor. He was interested in the mechanism of events rather than their ethical assessment. Though he was not without sympathy.

**SMITH:** Mr. Trevor, after your father's death, you were in communication with Holmes, and you provided him with a document that proved essential to understanding the full history. I refer to your father's own written account.

**TREVOR:** Yes. Among my father's papers was a lengthy statement, written in his own hand, which set out the whole of his history from his original troubles onwards. I believe he had written it against the possibility that the past might one day overtake him and he would need his account to be understood. When I read it, it explained everything I had never been able to ask him. I gave it to Holmes when he came to Donnithorpe after my father's death, and I asked him to make of it what he could. I was preparing to depart for the Terai — I needed to be away from England for a time — and I could not have imagined to take the document with me. I did not want to destroy it. I believed it should be in the hands of someone who would understand it.

**WATSON:** Holmes read it to me in its entirety. It is the kind of document that one does not easily forget.

**SMITH:** Doyle, can you give the audience an account of what the elder Mr. Trevor's confession contained?

**DOYLE:** I can, and gladly. The elder Mr. Trevor's real name was James Armitage. As a young man, he had been a clerk in a banking house, and had committed a serious offence, which resulted in his conviction and sentence of transportation. He was placed aboard a convict vessel called the Gloria Scott, bound for Australia. Aboard that ship, the convicts included a man of remarkable ability and force of character named Jack Prendergast, who had, by some means, contrived to have money conveyed to him aboard the vessel. This money allowed him to corrupt the ship's guards, and Prendergast organized a mutiny among the convicts, which succeeded.

**WATSON:** The account in the elder Mr. Trevor's confession of the mutiny itself is extraordinarily vivid. You sense the chaos and violence of it very strongly in the writing.

**DOYLE:** The mutiny having succeeded, the convicts found themselves in control of the ship. But their situation was precarious. A vessel appeared on the horizon, and it became clear that it was a naval ship. In the confusion and desperation that followed, the powder magazine on the Gloria Scott was ignited. The resulting explosion destroyed the vessel. Only a small number of men survived, escaping in a boat. Among them were James Armitage — who would become old Mr. Trevor — and a man named Beddoes, and the man who would be known as Hudson.

**TREVOR:** The survivors fabricated an account of themselves as castaways from a wreck, concealing entirely the nature of the ship they had been aboard and the circumstances of its destruction. They made their way to Australia, and in time my father came to England, adopted the name Trevor, established himself in Norfolk, and built the life that I grew up in.

**SMITH:** And Beddoes did the same?

**TREVOR:** Beddoes settled in Hampshire under his assumed name, yes. The two men had an agreement, as I understand it from my father's account, to maintain absolute silence about the past and to keep no connection with one another that might draw attention. For many years it worked. And then Hudson found them.

**WATSON:** Hudson had apparently made his way through various misfortunes and eventually fixed upon the two men as a source of support, knowing as he did the full truth of who they were and what the Gloria Scott had been. He had the essential qualification of the blackmailer: information that could destroy those who possessed what he lacked.

**SMITH:** I want to ask Holmes — through Watson, since Holmes is not here to speak for himself — about his own reflection on this as his first case. He has described it to you, Watson. What did he make of it?

**WATSON:** Holmes was careful to note that the term 'case' is perhaps somewhat generous, in that he did not solve anything in the sense of bringing a culprit to justice. He observed, and he listened, and after the elder Mr. Trevor's death he read and interpreted the confession. But the persons most directly responsible for events — Hudson, and Beddoes, and the whole dark history of the Gloria Scott — were beyond the reach of any action by that point. What the episode gave Holmes, he told me, was not a solved case but a confirmed method. He saw, for the first time, that his habit of reading men from small details had practical consequences in the real world, that it could penetrate secrets which their holders believed perfectly safe, and that the secrets thus revealed were not trivial things but could bear upon life and death. He said that the experience settled something in his mind about what he was for.

**DOYLE:** That is rather beautifully put, Watson. I drew on those reflections very directly when I came to write the story. There is a passage in the published version in which Holmes reflects on the experience as the thing that first gave him a practical sense of his own abilities. But Watson has captured the spirit of it precisely.

**TREVOR:** I am glad to hear that Holmes found something useful in the wreckage of those events. For my own part, I have sometimes wondered whether calling upon him that summer, by way of an invitation to Donnithorpe, was the right thing to do. Holmes observed what he observed quite naturally, not by design, but it was his presence at Donnithorpe that shook my father so profoundly during that first encounter, and I have occasionally asked myself whether my father's subsequent decline might have been precipitated, at least in part, by the fright of it.

**WATSON:** I do not think you need hold yourself responsible for that, Mr. Trevor. The elder Mr. Trevor's past was not a house of cards waiting to be toppled by a single breath. It was a structure that Hudson had been actively undermining for some time before Holmes arrived. The causes were old and deep.

**TREVOR:** I am grateful for that, Watson. And I think it is probably true. Certainly by the time Holmes arrived, Hudson was already in the picture. The storm had been gathering regardless.

**SMITH:** Holmes, as I understand it, retained your father's written confession, Mr. Trevor?

**TREVOR:** He did, at my request. I had no wish to have it about me, and I believed Holmes was the right custodian for it. He has a respect for documents that is, one suspects, more reliable than his housekeeping in other respects, if Watson's accounts of Baker Street are to be credited.

**WATSON:** [smiling] I will not dispute the point.

**SMITH:** Doyle, in writing up this story, you were working from Watson's transcription of Holmes's account, supplemented by the confession. Was there any aspect of the narrative that presented particular challenges?

**DOYLE:** The structural challenge is the most obvious one. Watson tells us of a winter evening at Baker Street; Holmes tells Watson of his student days and his visit to Donnithorpe; and then a substantial portion of the narrative consists of the elder Mr. Trevor's own written account of the Gloria Scott, which Holmes reads aloud. It is a story within a story within a story. I was concerned that the reader might feel the ground shifting too many times beneath them. But in the event, I think it works, because the emotional core — the old man's confession, his account of himself as young James Armitage, frightened and desperate and caught up in catastrophe — carries a directness that cuts through the layering.

**WATSON:** When Holmes read that confession aloud to me, the layering disappeared entirely. You forget that you are sitting in Baker Street. You are on the Gloria Scott, in the darkness, with the convicts below and the guards above and Prendergast at the centre of everything.

**TREVOR:** My father wrote well. I did not know that about him until I read it. He was not a man who spoke much of himself or expressed himself freely in ordinary conversation. But in that document he wrote with the kind of clarity that you find in a person who has kept a thing locked up for so long that when it finally comes out, it comes out whole.

**SMITH:** I think that is a very perceptive observation, Mr. Trevor. One final matter before we open the floor. The name of the ship itself — the Gloria Scott. It has a certain quality to it. There is an irony in a ship with a name that suggests glory and achievement being the vessel of convicts and catastrophe.

**DOYLE:** I have always felt that the name contributes something to the atmosphere of the story. It has the sound of something that should have been great and was instead ruined. And the story is, at its heart, about a ruination and its long shadow.

**TREVOR:** My father never used the name aloud, in all the years I knew him. I never heard it spoken in our household. It was only from his written account that I learned the name of the ship at all. For him, I think, it existed in a kind of enforced silence; the way one does not name a thing that has the power to undo you.

**WATSON:** Holmes did not romanticize the name or the events surrounding it. He treated the Gloria Scott as he would treat any other fixed point in a set of historical data: as a fact to be verified, a reference against which subsequent events could be measured. But even Holmes, I think, was not entirely unmoved by the scale of what had happened aboard her. He was very quiet when he finished reading the confession.

**SMITH:** Gentlemen, I think we have covered a great deal of ground this afternoon, and I am conscious that we have an audience who may wish to address questions to our participants. Before we open that portion of the program, I want to express, on behalf of The Strand Magazine and on behalf of everyone in this room, our sincere gratitude to Mr. Victor Trevor for his willingness to speak openly about events that are, as he has said, not without considerable personal weight. Arthur, Watson, as ever, thank you for your contributions. I would say that today's seminar has illuminated a story that is, in many ways, unlike any other in the Holmes canon — not because it involves Holmes at the height of his powers, but precisely because it shows us the man before he had fully understood what those powers were, or what use he would one day make of them.

**DOYLE:** That is precisely what I have always found most valuable about it. It is the only window we have into Holmes before Baker Street, before Watson, before the whole apparatus of the consulting detective as the world now knows him. In that sense, the Gloria Scott is not just a story about a ship and a secret. It is a story about a beginning.

**WATSON:** And beginnings, as Holmes himself once remarked to me, are the most instructive things in the world to examine. You see in them what a man is before circumstance has finished shaping him.

**TREVOR:** I will say only this, in closing: that whatever Holmes became in the years after that summer at Donnithorpe, he was already, then, the most remarkable person I had ever encountered. A young man who could look at my father for five minutes and see, as if through a window, something that my father had spent the better part of his life concealing. There is a kind of loneliness in that gift, I sometimes think. But there is also, clearly, a great deal of use in it. The world is the better for it, on balance. I am the better for having known him.

**SMITH:** Thank you all. Ladies and gentlemen, we shall now take a brief interval before opening the floor to questions from the audience.

*Applause from the audience. The participants take water. Several members of the front row are observed leaning toward one another in animated discussion*

# The Musgrave Ritual

*First Published in May, 1893*
*Sponsored by The Strand Magazine*
*Meeting Room B, British Museum, London*

## The Twentieth Seminar

**Herbert Greenhough Smith** — The Strand Editor & Moderator
**Arthur Conan Doyle** — Author and Watson's Literary Agent
**Dr. John H. Watson** —Colleague and Biographer of Sherlock Holmes
**Mr. Reginald Musgrave** — Friend of Sherlock Holmes

Seminar Transcript

**SMITH:** Ladies and gentlemen, welcome to the twentieth in our series of commemorative seminars celebrating the remarkable casebook of Mr. Sherlock Holmes, presented here at the British Museum in the spring of this new century. I am Herbert Greenhough Smith, editor of The Strand Magazine, and it is my honour once again to serve as your moderator. With us today, as always, are Arthur Conan Doyle, who has given literary form to these adventures, and Dr. John H. Watson, without whose meticulous notes none of these accounts would exist. Our distinguished guest this afternoon is Mr. Reginald Musgrave, of Hurlstone in western Sussex, a gentleman whose family history lies at the very heart of today's story. Gentlemen, welcome, all of you.

**DOYLE:** Thank you, Smith. It is a pleasure to be here once more, and I must say that today's story is one that holds a particular fascination for me. It reaches back to a period well before Watson entered the picture — one of Holmes's earlier independent cases — and yet it touches upon history of the most ancient and remarkable kind.

**WATSON:** I must acknowledge straightaway that my position today is somewhat different from the usual. In most of our seminars, I have been able to speak from direct experience, having been present at the events under discussion. With the Musgrave affair, that is emphatically not the case. Holmes recounted the whole business to me himself, in Baker Street, at a time when I had grown rather impatient with the extraordinary state of disorder in which he kept his papers and documents. It was in the course of my attempting to bring some order to his collection of records that he drew out the Musgrave papers and told me the story.

**SMITH:** Which gives it a special quality, does it not? A story within a story, as it were.

**WATSON:** Precisely. And I recorded it as faithfully as I could from Holmes's own telling of it.

**SMITH:** Mr. Musgrave, I wonder if we might begin with you. You were the gentleman who first brought this matter to Mr. Holmes. How did that come about?

**MUSGRAVE:** Certainly. Holmes and I had been acquainted during our time at college. We were not in the same set, I should say — our paths crossed in the way that they do between men of different interests and temperaments — but I was aware, as many of us were, that Holmes possessed quite unusual gifts of observation and analysis. By the time the trouble descended upon Hurlstone, he had already established himself as what I understood him to describe as a consulting detective, the only one of his kind. I therefore went directly to him in London. The affair had left me with a servant dead and a maidservant missing, and I confess I was quite at my wits' end.

**SMITH:** Before we reach those terrible events, would you describe Hurlstone for us, and the circumstances that led to the dismissal of your butler, Brunton?

**MUSGRAVE:** Hurlstone is the oldest inhabited building in the county. My family has held the property for several generations, and there is much about it — the old wing in particular — that is ancient beyond easy reckoning. The house is built upon a considerable estate. As for Brunton — he had been with us for some years and was, I must be frank, the most capable butler I have ever known or am likely to know. The man was of remarkable appearance, well-made and handsome, and his abilities were such that he had served not only as butler but had at various times acted almost as a general jack of all trades. He spoke several languages, played various instruments, and possessed a fund of information that would not have disgraced a man who had received the finest education. That said, his character was not without its shadows.

**SMITH:** In what respect?

**MUSGRAVE:** He had what I can only call a weakness where women were concerned. Among the female servants of the household, there had been difficulties of that kind on more than one occasion. But the immediate cause of his dismissal was something quite different. I came upon him late one night in the library. He was at my desk with a candle beside him, and he was reading from a document that had been locked away in the bureau. That document was the Musgrave Ritual.

**SMITH:** Arthur, perhaps you might describe the Ritual for those in our audience who are not familiar with the story?

**DOYLE:** With pleasure. The Musgrave Ritual, as Holmes encountered it, was an old document — a collection of questions and answers, passed down through the generations of the Musgrave family. The questions and their prescribed responses had been repeated by each heir upon coming of age, as a kind of family ceremony. The family themselves had lost any clear understanding of its meaning and regarded it simply as an old custom, though they preserved it carefully. The questions concerned certain features of the estate — an oak, an elm, a particular position relative to the old hall — together with rather cryptic references to an unnamed object.

**WATSON:** I recall from Holmes's own description that the Ritual referred to an oak, asking where it stood and what should be done in relation to it. There were compass directions and measured paces involved. And there were questions about what was to be given and why, with answers touching upon trust.

**MUSGRAVE:** That is correct. I knew the Ritual by heart, as every Musgrave before me had done, but I had never thought to interpret it as anything more than a ceremony. That Brunton had thought otherwise was evident from the manner in which he was studying it when I discovered him.

**SMITH:** And you dismissed him on the spot?

**MUSGRAVE:** I told him that he must leave my service immediately. He begged to be allowed a week, pleading some private matter of arrangement, and I conceded that much. It was within that week — indeed, within a very few days — that he disappeared.

**SMITH:** Dr. Watson, how did Holmes respond when Mr. Musgrave laid all of this before him?

**WATSON:** As Holmes described it to me, his immediate interest was seized by the Ritual itself. You must understand that Holmes is seldom more energized than when confronted with an old puzzle — something that has sat unsolved for generations. He saw at once, or very quickly, that the Ritual was not a mere family eccentricity but a set of directions, carefully encoded, leading to something of significance. He asked Mr. Musgrave for the precise wording of the document, which Musgrave was able to provide from memory, and then he set about applying his methods to it.

**SMITH:** Mr. Musgrave, when Holmes arrived at Hurlstone, what were the conditions he found?

**MUSGRAVE:** Brunton had been missing for several days. What made matters still more complicated was that one of the housemaids, a Welsh girl by the name of Rachel Howells, had also disappeared shortly afterward. She had been unwell — in a nervous state — in the days following Brunton's disappearance, and one night she was simply gone. We found some traces of her near the lake at the edge of the grounds, and a number of articles that had apparently been dragged through the garden. That was all. The police had been to the house and could make nothing of it.

**SMITH:** A double disappearance. Most alarming.

**MUSGRAVE:** Extremely so. And there was a particular circumstance surrounding Rachel Howells that had a bearing on the matter. She had previously been Brunton's sweetheart — or so it was understood among the servants. But Brunton had, in the way that apparently came naturally to him, abandoned her in favor of another woman, Janet Tregellis, the daughter of the head game-keeper. Rachel had taken it very badly, as one would expect, and she was not a woman of an even temper even under ordinary circumstances.

**WATSON:** Holmes had this from Mr. Musgrave, and it immediately put him on the right track, I think — or rather, it confirmed a direction he was already inclined to take.

**SMITH:** Let us turn to Holmes's decipherment of the Ritual itself. Dr. Watson, could you walk us through his reasoning?

**WATSON:** Holmes explained it to me step by step. The Ritual specified an elm and an oak, and paced directions from each in terms of compass bearings and numbers of steps. The oak, however, had long since been felled — it had been struck by lightning, I believe, and the stump alone remained. Holmes noted the stump and took measurements from it as the original starting point. In conducting his survey, he determined the length of the shadow cast by the elm at a particular time, using the height of the tree and the angle of the sun, and then paced off the distances specified in the Ritual — north by a certain number, east by a certain number, south by a further number, and so on. The final instruction was to go under — that is, underground. And beneath the earth at the point thus indicated, he found a stone slab serving as a door.

**SMITH:** Mr. Musgrave, were you present when Holmes conducted this survey?

**MUSGRAVE:** I was. I accompanied him over the grounds while he paced and calculated. I confess I watched him with some mixture of hope and skepticism. I had walked that ground hundreds of times and seen only the ordinary features of my own estate. To watch Holmes look at those same features with an entirely different kind of attention was instructive.

**SMITH:** And what was found when the stone slab was raised?

**MUSGRAVE:** An underground chamber of some kind — it appeared to be an old vault or cellar, of considerable age. And in it we found Brunton. He was dead.

**SMITH:** I imagine that was a profound shock.

**MUSGRAVE:** It was. Whatever his faults — and they were real enough — Brunton had been a part of the household for years. To find him there, in that dark place beneath my own grounds, was deeply disturbing. Holmes determined that he had been enclosed there and had died from want of air.

**WATSON:** Holmes's reconstruction of events, as he told me, was as follows. Brunton had at some point decoded the Ritual — or gone a considerable way toward doing so — and had gone down into the vault, presumably to retrieve whatever was hidden there. He had not gone alone. Holmes believed that Rachel Howells had assisted him, perhaps under some form of coercion or persuasion, in raising the heavy stone slab that served as the entrance. Whatever understanding had existed between them, it did not survive the occasion. Holmes concluded that Rachel, remembering how Brunton had treated her — that she had been cast aside in favor of another woman — had lowered the stone slab and left him to his fate.

**SMITH:** A grim and terrible revenge.

**WATSON:** Quite. And Holmes noted that the stone was far too heavy for one person to lift alone, which was why Brunton had required an accomplice in the first place. Having served that purpose, Rachel became — in Holmes's view — his executioner.

**MUSGRAVE:** Rachel was found wandering on the far side of the grounds some time later. She was in a very disturbed state and never gave a coherent account of what had occurred. She had been seen near the lake on the night of her disappearance, and items found there suggested something had been thrown into the water. Holmes recovered what could be found in the lake — it proved to be a linen bag containing what appeared to be old pebbles or stones — and he drew the obvious conclusion that she had disposed of evidence.

**SMITH:** But the linen bag was not the primary discovery in the vault, was it? There was something else.

**MUSGRAVE:** There was. In the vault, Holmes found a wooden box, very old, and within it certain objects. The metal work was badly corroded and some pieces had clearly disintegrated over time, but what remained was identifiable. Holmes told me what it was, and I confess that at first I could scarcely believe it.

**SMITH:** Dr. Watson, what was Holmes's identification of the object?

**WATSON:** Holmes told Mr. Musgrave — and told me subsequently in his recounting of the case — that the contents of the box were the ancient crown of the Kings of England. He connected it to the period of the Civil War and to the fact that the Musgraves had been among those families loyal to the Crown. His reasoning was that the Ritual had been devised as a means of preserving the knowledge of where this object had been hidden, and passing it down through the family in a form that would be meaningless to any outsider who might happen upon it.

**MUSGRAVE:** It was a considerable thing to take in. That my family had, through all those generations, been reciting those questions and answers without any understanding of what they referred to — that the entire history of the Ritual had been, in essence, a method of safekeeping passed from father to son — was remarkable. Holmes kept the crown, as it were, in his Baker Street rooms for a time, in that rather extraordinary collection of his. I would not have had it any other way, under the circumstances.

**SMITH:** That is an intriguing point. He kept the crown himself?

**WATSON:** He did, yes. Holmes's rooms at that period — this was before our time together at Baker Street — were rather notable for the state of organized chaos that prevailed in them. He had a horror of destroying papers and a rather eccentric approach to cataloguing his records. When I began to attempt some order on the documents at Baker Street, he drew out the Musgrave papers from an old wooden box — a battered tin box, I believe it was — and told me the story. I sometimes think that half of what Holmes recounted to me came about because I tried to tidy up his rooms.

*Laughter from the audience*

**SMITH:** Arthur, when Watson's account of this case was brought to you, what struck you most about it as a story?

**DOYLE:** What struck me above all was the architecture of it — the fact that the mystery had two entirely separate layers. There was the modern mystery of the disappearances, which any competent detective might have attempted to untangle, and then there was this older puzzle embedded within it: the Ritual itself, which reached back into history. To solve the modern problem, Holmes had first to solve the ancient one. I found that layering of the story to be quite magnificent. And the Ritual itself is one of the most arresting devices in the whole series of stories, I think. It reads almost like a catechism or a liturgy, and yet it is a practical document.

**SMITH:** Mr. Musgrave, looking back — and I appreciate this may be a delicate question — do you feel that Holmes's conclusions regarding Rachel Howells and what she did to Brunton were correct?

**MUSGRAVE:** I think the evidence pointed where it pointed, and Holmes's ability to read evidence was not something one questioned lightly. Rachel was in a disturbed state when she was found, and she never gave an account that would have clarified matters. What Brunton said to her, what he promised or threatened, I cannot say. What I can say is that she was a woman who had been treated badly, and that what ultimately befell Brunton was — well, I leave others to make what moral judgment they will. It was not a matter I ever felt comfortable adjudicating.

**WATSON:** Holmes himself was not in the business of moral judgment, in the ordinary sense. He determined what had happened and why. The justice of it, or the absence of justice, was not his primary concern.

**DOYLE:** And in writing the story up from Watson's notes, I found that same quality one I wanted to preserve. There is something deliberately unresolved about the fate of Rachel Howells — she is found, she is in a nervous state, she never fully explains herself. The reader is left to draw their own conclusions.

**SMITH:** Dr. Watson, is there anything in Holmes's own conduct of this case that stays with you particularly?

**WATSON:** What Holmes described to me, and what lodged in my mind, was his account of pacing out those directions on the Musgrave estate — using the measurements he derived from the elm tree and the stub of the old oak, finding the precise spot where the calculations led him, and then discovering the stone. There is something almost theatrical about it. He was enacting instructions that had been set down, one assumed, during the Civil War — following directions that someone had gone to extraordinary lengths to encode and preserve. One imagines the original creator of the Ritual, whatever loyal Musgrave it was, devising these questions and answers in the knowledge that the times were dangerous and that concealment was necessary. Holmes was, in a sense, completing a task that had been left unfinished for centuries.

**SMITH:** That is beautifully put, Watson.

**MUSGRAVE:** It is how I felt watching him. I should add — and perhaps this has not been noted elsewhere — that Holmes was quite precise about the question of the oak. He did not overlook the fact that the stump remained and made use of it. Many people, I think, upon finding that the oak referred to in the document was gone, would simply have been defeated. Holmes was not.

**SMITH:** As a final note before we open the floor to questions from our audience: Mr. Musgrave, do you feel that coming to Holmes was the right course of action, even given the discoveries that were made?

**MUSGRAVE:** Without question. Brunton would have been found eventually, and the circumstances would have remained obscure, and the history of that vault and what it contained would never have been known. Holmes gave me the truth of what had happened in my own house, on my own land. That it was an uncomfortable truth is beyond argument. But discomfort and ignorance are two quite different things, and I have always preferred the former to the latter.

**SMITH:** A sentiment, I think, that Mr. Sherlock Holmes would entirely endorse. That brings us to the end of this seminar. On behalf of The Strand Magazine and the British Museum, I want to thank you for coming.

*Sustained applause*

# The Reigate Squire

*First Published in June, 1893*
*Sponsored by The Strand Magazine*
*Meeting Room B, British Museum, London*

## The Twenty-First Seminar

**Herbert Greenhough Smith** — The Strand Editor & Moderator
**Arthur Conan Doyle** — Author and Watson's Literary Agent
**Dr. John H. Watson** —Colleague and Biographer of Sherlock Holmes
**Colonel Hayter** — Watson's Friend
**Inspector Forrester** — Inspector in the Surrey Constabulary

Seminar Transcript

**SMITH:** Ladies and gentlemen, good afternoon, and welcome to the twenty-first in our series of commemorative seminars on the cases of Mr. Sherlock Holmes. I am Herbert Greenhough Smith, editor of The Strand Magazine, and it falls to me, as always, to serve as your moderator for this afternoon's proceedings. We are gathered, as we have been these many pleasant Saturdays and Sundays past, in this magnificent room of the British Museum, and I believe I may say without fear of contradiction that our audience has grown rather appreciably with each successive installment. That, I think, is a testament not merely to public curiosity about Mr. Holmes, but to the extraordinary stories which Dr. Watson has so faithfully set before us, and which Arthur has so brilliantly rendered into the prose we have all come to treasure. Today we turn our attention to the case known as "The Adventure of the Reigate Squire," a singular affair which took Dr. Watson and Mr. Holmes into the Surrey countryside, to the village of Reigate, and which involved a burglary, a murder, a scrap of paper no larger than a man's palm, and a deduction of such startling precision that I confess it made me shiver when I first read it in Dr. Watson's notes. Joining Arthur and Dr. Watson today, we have three gentlemen without whom this story cannot be properly told: Colonel Hayter, whose hospitality provided the very setting in which the adventure began; Mr. Acton, whose household was subjected to a most peculiar burglary; and Inspector Forrester of the Surrey Constabulary, who had charge of the official investigation. Gentlemen, welcome, and thank you for making the journey today.

**HAYTER:** It is a pleasure, Mr. Smith. I will confess that when The Strand first wrote to me requesting my presence, I very nearly declined. I am not a man who courts attention. But then I thought of Holmes — of what he accomplished that April — and I decided that if this gathering serves in any way to honor him, I should be very glad to be part of it.

**ACTON:** I echo the Colonel's sentiments. I am, by nature, a private man, and the events of that week touched upon matters — namely, the longstanding lawsuit between my family and the Cunninghams — which I would ordinarily prefer not to discuss in public. Yet the thing is done now, the law has had its way, and I see no harm in speaking honestly about what occurred.

**FORRESTER:** And I am simply pleased to be here. I have appeared before audiences in the course of my professional duties, but never quite like this. I will say only that the Reigate case, as we call it in the Surrey Constabulary, remains among the most instructive I have encountered, and not for any reason that reflects well upon my own powers of detection. Mr. Holmes rather put us all in the shade.

**SMITH:** Ha! A frank admission, Inspector, and one that I suspect will endear you to our audience. Now, Dr. Watson, let us begin at the beginning, as we always do. How did this adventure come to find you and Mr. Holmes in Reigate at all?

**WATSON:** The circumstances preceding our visit were, I must say, rather alarming — at least to me as Holmes's physician and friend. Holmes had thrown himself with extraordinary energy into the case concerning the Netherlands-Sumatra Company and the colossal schemes of the Baron Maupertuis. It was a matter which engaged all of Europe, and Holmes's exertions upon it had been prodigious. When at last it was resolved, the reaction upon him was severe. He had overworked his constitution very grievously, and for some time I was not without anxiety on his behalf. His doctors in France were quite insistent that he must have rest.

**DOYLE:** I should say here, for those who may not have read the story closely, that this collapse of Holmes's was no small affliction. When

Watson has occasion to describe Holmes in a state of genuine physical debility, it is because the man truly had pushed himself to the very limit of what a human constitution can sustain. The case of Baron Maupertuis had demanded weeks of the most intense mental labor, and Holmes paid the price for it.

**WATSON:** Quite so. And it was then that Colonel Hayter — with whom I had served, or rather, whom I had attended, in Afghanistan — very kindly offered the use of his home near Reigate. He had come under my care during that period, and we had remained on the friendliest terms since. When I suggested to Holmes that we might take Hayter up on his invitation, Holmes agreed readily enough. He was in no condition to disagree with anything at that moment, which is a state of affairs that does not usually persist for very long with Sherlock Holmes.

**SMITH:** Colonel Hayter, what was your impression of Mr. Holmes when he arrived at your home?

**HAYTER:** He was not well. That was plain from the moment Watson helped him out of the carriage. He was pale and thinner than I should have liked to see a man, and there was a listlessness about him that struck me as quite out of keeping with the reputation Watson had led me to expect. Watson had spoken of Holmes often — with great admiration, I should say — and I had formed a picture in my mind of a man of ferocious energy. What I saw instead was a man who needed a comfortable chair, a warm fire, and a long stretch of days with absolutely nothing whatever to demand his attention.

**WATSON:** And he was getting on rather well, in fact, until the business of the Reigate burglaries intruded itself. The country air seemed to be doing him genuine good. He was sleeping better, eating reasonably well — Holmes is never what one would call a hearty eater — and I had real hopes of a full recovery, provided nothing arose to agitate him.

**SMITH:** And then something arose to agitate him. Mr. Acton, perhaps you would describe for us what occurred at your house?

**ACTON:** Yes. It was a strange business, and strange not chiefly because a burglary had taken place — one can understand a burglar well enough — but because of what the burglar chose to take. My house had indeed been broken into, and when I conducted a careful inventory of what had been disturbed, the list of missing items struck me and everyone else as perfectly incomprehensible. The intruder had taken a ball of twine, a candle, a glass paperweight, some loose screws, a calendar, an ivory letter-weight, a small novel, and a miniature of a lady painted on ivory. There was no obvious logic to it. These were not the valuables a competent thief would seek out.

**FORRESTER:** Which is precisely what made it so puzzling from the investigative standpoint. I had seen burglaries of all varieties in my years with the Surrey Constabulary, but nothing quite like this. The articles taken were, in the aggregate, of virtually no monetary value. And yet the burglar had gone to the trouble of entering the premises, moving through the house with some deliberation, and removing these particular things. It made no sense — or rather, it made no sense on any theory I could construct at the time.

**SMITH:** Colonel Hayter, at what point did you bring this matter to Mr. Holmes's attention?

**HAYTER:** I was in a somewhat delicate position, because Watson had been quite firm on the question of Holmes resting and not being drawn into anything that might tax him. But the news of the burglary at Acton's place was circulating in the neighborhood, and Inspector Forrester called on me — we were acquainted — and mentioned it in the course of conversation. Holmes happened to be present. I believe I had expected Holmes to show no more than the polite interest of a convalescent with nothing better to do. What I observed instead was something quite different. A gleam came into his eyes.

**WATSON:** I noticed it as well, and I confess my heart sank somewhat. I had seen that gleam before, and I knew perfectly well what it meant.

**FORRESTER:** I shall be candid: I was not entirely at ease with Mr. Holmes taking an interest in the matter. Not from any personal hostility, you understand, but simply because it is never entirely comfortable, as a professional officer, to have a private individual — however celebrated — involve himself in one's case. But Colonel Hayter vouched for him, and in any event Holmes had a way of making it very clear that he intended to be involved whether one welcomed it or not. So I was glad enough of his company, and I introduced him to Mr. Acton.

**ACTON:** Yes, and I remember my impression of him quite well. He seemed to me, when first introduced, a man who was not yet fully himself — Watson had said as much, that he was recovering from a great strain — and yet there was, even then, a precision in his questions that told you immediately you were dealing with no ordinary mind. He asked me about the items that had been taken with a specificity that surprised me. He seemed less interested in the fact of the burglary than in the exact nature of what had been removed and from which rooms.

**SMITH:** Dr. Watson, the story then takes a darker turn. Overnight, a murder occurs. Would you describe those circumstances?

**WATSON:** Yes. That same night, or rather in the early hours of the morning following, William Kirwan, who was a coachman in the employ of the Cunninghams — the Cunninghams being a family of some standing in the neighborhood, consisting of old Mr. Cunningham and his son Alec — William Kirwan was found shot dead in the yard of the Cunningham property. The alarm was raised by the Cunninghams themselves, who reported that they had heard the shot, looked from their windows, and observed a man fleeing. According to their account, this unknown man had been attempting to break in, and Kirwan had disturbed him.

**FORRESTER:** That was the account they gave me, yes. And on the surface of it, one could see a pattern — a burglar operating in the district, first at Mr. Acton's, then at the Cunninghams', and Kirwan the unfortunate victim of a chance encounter. The natural interpretation was that the two events were connected, and that whoever had burgled Acton's house had now turned to violence. I will say in my own defense that this was not an unreasonable hypothesis on the evidence available to me at that moment.

**SMITH:** Of course, Inspector. And what altered that hypothesis?

**FORRESTER:** Mr. Holmes altered it. The fragment of paper altered it. Holmes drew my attention to the fact that Kirwan was clutching in his dead hand a scrap of paper. It was a torn piece of a note, and upon it were written the words: 'at quarter to twelve learn what.' Holmes was immediately struck by this, and it was from the study of that small piece of paper that everything else unraveled.

**WATSON:** Holmes was fascinated by the note from the instant he saw it. He held it up and examined it with the most intense concentration. I was watching his face, and I could see that he was forming conclusions with extraordinary rapidity. He said very little at the time, which I have learned over the years usually means that he has seen a great deal.

**DOYLE:** The crucial insight, as Watson's notes made clear to me when I came to write the story, was Holmes's recognition that the fragment had been written by two different hands — not one. This is the heart of the deduction, and it is worth dwelling upon. The note appeared at first glance to be a unified document, but Holmes perceived that the letters composing the words 'at quarter to twelve' had been formed by one person, and the words 'learn what' by another. The two hands were distinct in their characteristics, and he further deduced from those characteristics that they belonged to a father and son respectively.

**SMITH:** That is a remarkable piece of analysis. Dr. Watson, how did Holmes go about demonstrating this to those present?

**WATSON:** He asked Inspector Forrester and myself to look very closely at the handwriting in the different parts of the note, and to observe the differences in the formation of certain letters. He pointed out that the writer of 'at quarter to twelve' formed his letters in one manner, with particular characteristics I need not enumerate at length here, while the writer of 'learn what' used a different hand altogether. Holmes concluded that the first writer was an elderly man, from the slightly trembling quality of some strokes, and the second a younger man of some education. He was quite certain of it.

**FORRESTER:** I will confess that even after Holmes pointed out the distinctions, I was not immediately persuaded that they supported such a sweeping conclusion. To my eye, it was simply a scrap of paper with some words on it. But Holmes was adamant, and as events proved, he was right in every particular. Old Mr. Cunningham had written one portion, and his son Alec the other.

**SMITH:** Now, Mr. Acton, at this point in the investigation, were you made aware of how your burglary connected to the murder of Kirwan?

**ACTON:** Not immediately, no. It was only later, when the full truth came out, that I understood the connection — and it was a connection that touched upon matters I would rather had remained buried, though not for any discreditable reason on my part. There had been, for some time, a lawsuit between my family and the Cunninghams over certain property. The legal position was, I believe, entirely clear, and indeed the courts were in the process of confirming my claim. But the Cunninghams had an interest in finding certain documents that might affect the case. It was for the purpose of searching for those documents that they had broken into my house. The other articles they took were merely camouflage, to make it appear as though an ordinary thief had been at work.

**SMITH:** And William Kirwan — what was his role in all of this?

**WATSON:** Kirwan had seen the Cunninghams during the burglary at Acton's house, and he had been using that knowledge against them. He was, in short, making demands upon them. The Cunninghams, to rid themselves of this danger, devised the scheme of luring Kirwan to a meeting at night by means of that note, and then shooting him. They constructed the story of the fleeing burglar to explain away the gunshot and the death.

**FORRESTER:** And it was a scheme that might very well have succeeded, had it not been for Mr. Holmes. There was, I must acknowledge, no obvious reason at the outset to disbelieve the Cunninghams' account. They were men of respectable standing in the community, and the story of an intruder shot while attempting a burglary was entirely plausible given what had occurred at Acton's place the night before.

**SMITH:** Dr. Watson, the story contains an episode which I find among the most vivid in all the accounts you have given us — Mr. Holmes simulating a fainting fit. Would you describe what happened?

**WATSON:** It was extraordinary to witness. Holmes had perceived that the fragment of note found in Kirwan's hand was not the whole of it — that the rest of the note still existed, and that the Cunninghams were in possession of it. The complete note, if recovered, would prove conclusively that they had written to Kirwan and therefore had lured him to his death. Holmes needed to obtain the remainder without the Cunninghams understanding his purpose. And so, in the course of our visit to the

Cunninghams' house, when the moment was right, he suddenly appeared to collapse — to swoon quite away, as though the exertion had been too much for a man still recovering from illness. We all rushed to his aid, and in the confusion, Holmes palmed the fragment of note which the Cunninghams had been at some pains to conceal.

**HAYTER:** I was alarmed, I don't mind saying. I knew Holmes was not a well man, and for a moment I was not at all sure that the collapse was not genuine. Watson's expression was one of concern, which did nothing to reassure me. It was only afterwards, when Holmes sat up looking perfectly composed and produced the scrap of paper, that I understood what he had done.

**WATSON:** I was not entirely in his confidence about that move, I will admit. Holmes operates on the principle that the fewer people who know what he intends, the more convincing the performance. He was right, of course — the Cunninghams were wholly deceived — but it was rather hard on my nerves.

**DOYLE:** Watson's account of that moment in his notes was, if I may say so, exceptionally vivid, and I had very little need to embellish it. The image of Holmes suddenly falling to the ground, and then, moments later, sitting quietly and producing the recovered paper, is one that I think will remain with readers for a very long time.

**SMITH:** Inspector Forrester, I must ask you about the more dangerous episode that followed. Mr. Holmes was, if I understand the account correctly, physically attacked.

**FORRESTER:** He was. When it became clear to the Cunninghams that Holmes had seen through their deception — and Holmes, I must say, made it very clear, with that directness of his that leaves one in no doubt about what he knows — young Alec Cunningham turned violent. He had Holmes by the wrist, and the situation for a moment was genuinely dangerous. Holmes was not, at that period, in the physical condition he might ordinarily have been, and Alec Cunningham was a vigorous man. I intervened as quickly as I was able.

**HAYTER:** I had my revolver with me. I had brought it because — well, because one does not quite know what one will encounter when accompanying Sherlock Holmes into a situation of that nature, and I had had enough military experience to believe that being armed is generally preferable to being otherwise. When young Cunningham seized Holmes, I made it known that I had the weapon and that I was prepared to use it. That had a satisfactory effect upon the proceedings.

**WATSON:** Between Hayter's revolver and Forrester's professional authority, and my own assistance, we were able to secure both of the Cunninghams. Holmes, once freed, showed no particular signs of distress, though I examined him carefully afterwards and was not entirely satisfied with what I found. He had been handled roughly. But he was in remarkable spirits — which is always the way with Holmes when a case has concluded to his satisfaction.

**SMITH:** Arthur, you mentioned earlier the fragment of the note and the two hands. I wonder if you might elaborate a little more on that deduction for the benefit of our audience, because it seems to me the very core of the intellectual achievement in this case.

**DOYLE:** Certainly. The note, as recovered in pieces, constituted a message sent by the Cunninghams to Kirwan, appointing a time and place for the fatal meeting. The full text of the combined fragments established this. But Holmes's insight — gleaned from the fragment alone, before the rest was recovered — was to recognize that the note had been written by two people working together, and that those two people were of different generations. The older man's letters showed one set of characteristics, the younger man's another. From this, Holmes inferred that the two writers shared a close domestic connection and that they were acting in concert. The logical candidates, given everything else he had observed, were old Mr. Cunningham and his son Alec.

**WATSON:** It was a deduction that seems, in retrospect, to follow quite naturally. But at the time, when Holmes announced it, it struck me as a kind of conjuring trick. I had looked at the same scrap of paper and seen only words. Holmes looked at it and saw two men, their ages, their relationship, and their guilt.

**FORRESTER:** I have thought about it many times since. The lesson I drew from the experience — and I believe it has made me a better officer — is that one must never look at evidence and see only what one expects to see. I expected to see the product of a single hand because it did not occur to me to question the assumption. Holmes questioned everything, assumed nothing, and consequently saw what was actually there.

**SMITH:** Mr. Acton, you mentioned the lawsuit between yourself and the Cunninghams. Now that the matter has been resolved in the way that it has, do you find it strange to reflect that a legal dispute over property ultimately led to a murder?

**ACTON:** I find it deeply sobering. I want to be clear that I bear no personal satisfaction from how things ended. I have no wish to speak ill of the Cunninghams beyond what the facts of the case require. What I will say is that the lawsuit itself was entirely proper on my part, pursued through lawful means, and I had every confidence in the eventual outcome through the ordinary processes of the courts. The actions the Cunninghams took — the burglary, and then the terrible crime against that poor man Kirwan — were quite beyond anything a legal dispute could be said to justify or explain. And I am sorry that William Kirwan lost his life as a consequence of a chain of events that had its origin, however indirectly, in a disagreement that touched upon my affairs.

**SMITH:** That is graciously said, Mr. Acton. Colonel Hayter, looking back on those days in Reigate, what is your abiding impression of Sherlock Holmes as a man?

**HAYTER:** He is unlike anyone I have ever met, and I say that having met a great many men in unusual circumstances over the course of a long military career. What strikes me most is not his cleverness, which is of course remarkable, but his absolute concentration. When Holmes is engaged upon a problem, the rest of the world simply ceases to exist for him. He brings to bear the whole of his attention, without reservation, without distraction. I watched him that week, and the transformation from the exhausted, pallid man who had arrived in my drawing room to the alert, purposeful figure who took command of events at the Cunninghams' house was quite startling. The problem was, in a very real sense, the medicine that restored him.

**WATSON:** As a physician, I found that rather vexing at the time, and rather wonderful in retrospect. I had prescribed rest and quiet. Holmes found his restoration in precisely the opposite. It is not a prescription I would recommend universally, but for Holmes, it appeared to answer.

**SMITH:** Arthur, as you read Dr. Watson's notes on this case and prepared them for publication, was there any aspect of it that presented particular difficulties or that you found especially worthy of attention?

**DOYLE:** The handwriting analysis was the element that required the most care in the telling. A deduction that proceeds from physical evidence — from the characteristics of a person's handwriting — must be conveyed in such a way that the reader can follow the reasoning, or at least believe in it, without being made to feel that they are reading a treatise on handwriting. Watson's notes gave me the substance, but the presentation required some thought. I also found Holmes's simulated collapse a gift, in literary terms. It is a moment of theater — Holmes in the role of the helpless invalid, performing it to perfection precisely because he is normally so very far from helpless — and I think it illuminates something true about his character, namely that he is willing to appear whatever he needs to appear in the service of a goal.

**FORRESTER:** I should mention, since we are speaking of how the story presents itself, that I thought Arthur dealt very fairly with the police in this account. In some of the stories, I understand the official investigators do not emerge with a great deal of credit. Here, I think it is plain that I was working with incomplete information and doing what any competent officer would have done with what he had. It was Holmes who supplied what was missing.

**DOYLE:** The professional police are always men doing their best within the constraints of their methods, Inspector. I hope I have never suggested otherwise.

**SMITH:** Dr. Watson, is there anything about the case that you feel the published account does not fully capture? Anything that remains in the original notes that readers have not had the benefit of seeing?

**WATSON:** There is always more in the notes than makes its way into print. That is the nature of the thing. Arthur must make choices, and he makes them well — far better, I suspect, than I should make them myself. What the published account perhaps does not fully convey is the texture of those days at Hayter's house before the case began in earnest: the quietness of the Surrey countryside, the particular quality of the light on the hills, the sense of something approaching tranquility that Holmes was very nearly achieving. When the news of the burglary came in, and I saw that gleam return to his eyes, I felt almost a kind of grief for the rest that was not to be. Though I ought to have known, after all the years I had spent in Holmes's company, that rest and Sherlock Holmes are not natural companions.

**HAYTER:** He was welcome back at any time, I told him as much when he left. And I meant it. The peace of the neighborhood was somewhat disturbed by the events, but I find, looking back, that I do not regret any of it. One does not often have the chance to witness genius at work at such close quarters. It is a privilege, even when it is also rather alarming.

**SMITH:** That is a fitting note on which to draw our discussion toward its close. We have heard today from three men who found themselves, as the Colonel says, at close quarters with an extraordinary mind at a singular moment. Gentlemen, I thank you all — Colonel Hayter, Mr. Acton, Inspector Forrester — for your candor, your good humor, and your willingness to illuminate from the inside a case which has been very widely read and admired. And I thank, as always, Dr. Watson, who gave us the case in the first instance, and Arthur, who gave it to the world in the form in which we know it. I would add only this: that there is something in the affair of the Reigate Squire that seems to me peculiarly characteristic of Mr. Holmes at his finest. He came to that village a sick man, seeking nothing more than quiet and the restoration of his health. He found instead a mystery, and in the solving of it he found, by his own singular constitution, the very health he had been seeking. That, I think, tells us something important about Sherlock Holmes — not merely about his methods, but about the man himself. This seminar is now concluded. Good afternoon to you all.

*Sustained applause*

# The Crooked Man

*First Published in July, 1893*
*Sponsored by The Strand Magazine*
*Meeting Room B, British Museum, London*

**The Twenty-Second Seminar**

**Herbert Greenhough Smith** — The Strand Editor & Moderator
**Arthur Conan Doyle** — Author and Watson's Literary Agent
**Dr. John H. Watson** —Colleague and Biographer of Sherlock Holmes
**Colonel Hayter** — Watson's Friend
**Inspector Forrester** — Inspector in the Surrey Constabulary

Seminar Transcript

**SMITH:** Good afternoon, ladies and gentlemen, and welcome to the twenty-second installment of The Strand Magazine's Public Seminar Series, here in the magnificent surroundings of the British Museum. I am Herbert Greenhough Smith, Editor of The Strand Magazine, and it is my privilege once again to serve as your moderator. As always, we are joined by the author of the Sherlock Holmes stories, Arthur Conan Doyle, and by the man without whose case notes these chronicles could never have been written, Dr. John H. Watson. This afternoon's seminar concerns a story of particular gravity — a story of old soldiers, long-buried betrayal, and the relentless reach of a guilty conscience across the span of many years. The story in question is "The Adventure of the Crooked Man," and we are fortunate to have with us today three individuals who played central roles in those events: Mrs. Nancy Barclay, widow of Colonel James Barclay of the Royal Munsters; Mr. Henry Wood, formerly a corporal in that same regiment; and Major Murphy, also of the Royal Munsters, who first brought the matter to the attention of Mr. Sherlock Holmes. We extend our warmest welcome and our sincere gratitude to each of them for agreeing to speak with us this afternoon. It cannot have been an easy decision, and their willingness to revisit these painful events in a public forum is a testament to their courage and their generosity of spirit.

**SMITH:** Before we proceed to the events themselves, I should like to begin, as is our custom, with Dr. Watson. Doctor, would you be so kind as to set the scene for our audience? How did this case first come to your attention, and what were your initial impressions when Mr. Holmes described it to you?

**WATSON:** Certainly, Smith. I had not seen Holmes for some time — I had, of course, returned to my practice, and our meetings had become less frequent than in our Baker Street days. He came to me quite late one evening, in that energetic and purposeful manner he always assumed when a case had seized his interest, and announced that he had been visited by a Major Murphy of the Royal Munsters, who had come to seek his assistance in what he described as a matter of the utmost delicacy. A colonel of the regiment, one James Barclay, had been found dead in his study at Aldershot under circumstances that were, on the surface, deeply incriminating to his wife. Holmes had naturally agreed to travel to Aldershot at once, and he invited me to accompany him. I did so gladly. It was one of those cases that engaged every faculty, not merely because of the mystery of the locked room and the death itself, but because one quickly sensed that whatever lay at the heart of it had roots running very deep indeed.

**SMITH:** Thank you, Doctor. And Arthur — as you assembled Dr. Watson's notes into narrative form, what struck you most forcefully about this particular story?

**DOYLE:** What struck me was the classical quality of the tragedy, if I may put it that way. One finds this structure in the oldest stories the world possesses — the Book of Samuel, for instance, which is explicitly invoked in the tale itself. A man of ambition commits a terrible wrong against a comrade in order to win the woman he desires. He flourishes. He rises in the world. He believes the past to be safely buried. And then, after the passage of many years, the past returns to him in the flesh. The horror Colonel Barclay must have felt in that room — the horror of recognition — is not something I had to invent. It is written into the very bones of the case. What interested me as a writer was that Holmes arrives, characteristically, not to solve a murder but to demonstrate that no murder was committed at all. The crime at the root of the story occurred not in that study in Aldershot, but on a road near Bhurtee, India, nearly thirty years before.

**SMITH:** Beautifully put. Now, Major Murphy — you were the first to seek Mr. Holmes's assistance. Would you tell us what you knew of the situation when you travelled to Baker Street, and what it was about the circumstances that convinced you that outside help was required?

**MURPHY:** I shall try to be as straightforward as I can, Mr. Smith. Colonel Barclay had commanded the Royal Munsters for some years, and he was a man I respected greatly — a fine soldier, well liked by his men. He and Mrs. Barclay were regarded as a devoted couple by all who knew them, though I will confess that those of us in the regiment had observed that the Colonel was subject to occasional moods — fits of dark temper that came upon him seemingly without cause. Mrs. Barclay, too, had her own sorrows to bear, though she wore them quietly. When the news reached the mess that the Colonel had been found dead, and that Mrs. Barclay had been discovered unconscious in the same locked room, the whole affair had an appearance that was deeply troubling. The door had been found locked from the inside. The window was open. There was a club — a peculiar, heavy weapon — lying near the body. It was quite clear that Mrs. Barclay could not have locked the door from the inside and then passed through it. Yet to a casual observer, the scene might suggest that some quarrel had taken place between husband and wife. I knew that the circumstances required a mind sharper than my own, and Mr. Holmes had a considerable reputation. I went to Baker Street the following morning.

**SMITH:** And Holmes received you promptly, I take it?

**MURPHY:** He did, and I can tell you he was a remarkable man to speak with. Before I had told him a great deal, he was already putting questions to me that I had not thought to ask myself. He was particularly interested in the nature of the room, in the position of the key, and in a report that had reached me from one of the servants — that some manner of strange creature had been seen in the vicinity of the house that evening. A dark, swift, writhing thing, they said. I confess that detail had struck me as the fancy of a frightened woman, but Holmes treated it with the greatest seriousness.

**WATSON:** It was the mongoose, of course — Teddy. Mr. Wood's creature. Holmes deduced its nature almost at once from the description.

**MURPHY:** Yes. Though none of us knew it then.

**SMITH:** Dr. Watson, Holmes was also quite interested in the history of the regiment, was he not? He asked Major Murphy certain questions about the past?

**WATSON:** He was interested in the career of Colonel Barclay — particularly in how he had risen to his rank. The Major told us that Barclay had enlisted as a private, that he had risen through the ranks with quite extraordinary speed, and that the step that launched him upward had been his conduct at the relief of Bhurtee during the Indian Mutiny. Holmes received this information with great attention. He was already forming the shape of the thing, I think, even at that early stage.

**SMITH:** We shall come to Bhurtee in due course. But first I wish to turn to Mrs. Barclay, because the audience will wish to hear from her directly about the evening of her husband's death. Mrs. Barclay, I recognize that this remains an acutely painful subject, and we are all grateful for your willingness to address it. Can you tell us, in your own words, what occurred on that evening?

**BARCLAY:** I will do my best, Mr. Smith. That afternoon I had been walking with a friend — Miss Morrison, who accompanied me on charitable visits for our Guild — and it was on our return that I encountered Henry Wood. After so many years, I confess I nearly did not recognize him at first. His appearance — his posture, his walk — had been so altered by what was done to him. But when I looked into his face, I knew him at once. Henry Wood. A man I had known in the old days in India, when James was still a sergeant and I was a young woman who had not yet fully understood what kind of man I had married. Henry spoke briefly with me. He told me where he was lodging, and I understood — though perhaps I did not fully admit it to myself — that the time of reckoning had arrived. That evening, when I returned home, something had settled over me. I confronted my husband. I told him that I had seen Henry Wood. I told him that I knew — that I had long suspected, though never permitted myself to know with certainty — what he had done at Bhurtee. What he had done to Henry.

**SMITH:** And how did your husband receive that?

**BARCLAY:** He was — he became very agitated. He did not deny it. I think by then he was beyond denial. There was a look in his face that I can only describe as the look of a man who has been waiting, for thirty years, for a knock at the door that he always knew would come. We quarreled bitterly. I used words — I used a name — that I am not proud of, though I do not retract the comparison I made. And then Henry appeared at the French window.

**SMITH:** Henry Wood appeared at the window while you and your husband were quarreling?

**BARCLAY:** He did. I had not sent for him; I do not think he came because of me, particularly. He came because he too had reached the end of something — some long journey, not merely from India, but inside himself. He had carried what was done to him for nearly thirty years, and when he saw me that afternoon I believe it broke open in him, all of it. He came to face James. And James — when he saw him — when he saw Henry's face, that ruined face, and knew what he was looking upon — he gave a great cry and fell. He was dead before I could reach him. Henry fled. I — I fainted. I cannot tell you precisely how long I lay there before the servants raised the alarm.

**SMITH:** Thank you, Mrs. Barclay. That must have required considerable fortitude to recount. Mr. Wood — you have heard Mrs. Barclay's account of that evening. Is there anything you wish to add or to clarify from your own perspective?

**WOOD:** I would say only that she has told it true. I am not a man who is easy to look upon, Mr. Smith. I know what I appear to be to a stranger's eyes. The years I spent in captivity, after Barclay betrayed me to the Sepoys at Bhurtee, did things to my body that cannot be undone. I walked at a crouch. My appearance became such that I could make a living only as a travelling showman — and that is what I did, for many years, with my mongoose Teddy and the other creature I carried. I had not intended to come back to England to do harm to anyone. What would have been the purpose? Barclay had risen high. He had his rank, his reputation, his comfortable life. And I — I had survived. I had my creature for company and the open road. But when I came to Aldershot and I saw Nancy — Mrs. Barclay — in the street, something in me could not let it pass. I did not go to that house to do violence. I went to stand in front of him and let him see what his treachery had made of me. That is all I wanted. For him to see.

**SMITH:** And you could not have anticipated that the shock of seeing you would prove fatal to him?

**WOOD:** No. Though if I had anticipated it — I am not certain it would have altered what I did. I am not proud to say that. But I think it is the truth, and I will not pretend otherwise before this audience.

**SMITH:** I appreciate your candor, Mr. Wood. Arthur, the moral weight of this case is quite considerable, is it not? Holmes himself arrives at a conclusion — that no murder has been committed — but the ethical questions surrounding Colonel Barclay's original act of betrayal seem to hang over everything.

**DOYLE:** They do, and I think that is precisely what gives the story its distinction. Holmes solves the mechanical puzzle swiftly and satisfyingly — the locked room, the strange creature, the position of the key, the cause of death. But the deeper puzzle — the question of justice, of whether Colonel Barclay's death constituted, in some providential sense, a settling of accounts — that is a puzzle Holmes declines to adjudicate. He is not in the business of moral philosophy. His role is to determine the facts. What the facts mean, and what weight we assign to Barclay's original crime against Wood, is a question the reader must answer for himself.

**WATSON:** Holmes did remark that Colonel Barclay, had he lived, might have faced serious consequences for what he did at Bhurtee — though how one would prosecute such a matter, after so many years, is another question entirely.

**SMITH:** Let us return, then, to Bhurtee, because I think many in our audience will wish to understand precisely what occurred there. Mr. Wood, would you take us back to that time, and explain, as plainly as you are able, what Sergeant Barclay did and what the consequences were for you?

**WOOD:** I will, though it is not a comfortable thing to speak of. We were at Bhurtee during the Mutiny. It was a desperate business — a garrison cut off, in danger of being overwhelmed. There were those inside who needed to get word out to the relief column. I was sent — or I volunteered, I am no longer entirely certain which — to slip through the enemy lines and make contact. Sergeant Barclay knew my route. He and I had been friends — or so I believed. We had grown up in the same part of the country. We were rivals, I suppose, for Nancy's affections, though I thought it was a friendly rivalry between comrades. He told me he wished me well. And then he informed the enemy of the route I would take. I was captured before I had gone half a mile.

**SMITH:** And you understood, at the time of your capture, what had happened? That you had been betrayed?

**WOOD:** Not immediately. One does not leap to that conclusion about a man one has called a friend. It was only later — much later, in captivity, with a great deal of time to think — that I understood it. There was no other way the enemy could have known my route. And once I understood it, I also understood why he had done it. With me gone — dead, or as good as dead — the path was clear for him. And so it proved. He distinguished himself in the relief. He rose rapidly. He married Nancy. He became, eventually, Colonel Barclay of the Royal Munsters. And I became what you see before you.

**SMITH:** Mrs. Barclay — you said a moment ago that you had long suspected what your husband had done. When did that suspicion first take hold in you?

**BARCLAY:** I cannot point to a single moment. It was more like a fog that gathered slowly, over years. James changed after we married. He became — he was subject to terrors in the night. Conscience, perhaps. There were things he would not speak of. The name of Henry Wood was never mentioned in our house — never, in all our years together. A man does not avoid a name so intentionally unless the name carries a great weight of guilt. And there were small things, over many years, that did not quite fit together. I told myself I was imagining it. A woman in my position — a colonel's wife — does not easily permit herself to look directly at such a possibility. But it was there, always, underneath.

**SMITH:** Dr. Watson, when Holmes spoke to the housekeeper — Miss Mason, I believe — and to the servants, what information did he gather about the events immediately prior to the death?

**WATSON:** The housekeeper had heard the voices of Colonel and Mrs. Barclay quarreling, which was quite unusual in itself, as by all accounts the Barclays were known for their domestic harmony. She heard Mrs. Barclay cry out a name — the name David — which struck the housekeeper as strange, as that was not the Colonel's name. Holmes, of course, understood the reference at once. It was the reproach of a woman who had come to understand, at last, the full nature of the wrong her husband had committed — who saw in him the mirror of King David, who sent Uriah the Hittite to the front of the battle to die, so that David might take Uriah's wife. The parallel was exact and devastating. Barclay had sent Wood to what he believed would be his death, for precisely the same reason.

**SMITH:** A remarkable piece of reasoning on Holmes's part. Arthur, how did Holmes ultimately reconstruct the sequence of events in the room itself? The locked door had at first suggested to the police that Mrs. Barclay must have been responsible for her husband's death.

**DOYLE:** The police had formed a theory that was, on the surface, not unreasonable. The room was locked from the inside. Only Mrs. Barclay was present. The Colonel was dead. The key was found upon the floor near Mrs. Barclay. The conclusion that she had killed him and then, in some fit of disordered feeling, had collapsed, and seemed to follow. Holmes dismantled this theory with characteristic thoroughness. He noted the open window. He observed that the strange creature reported by the servant — Teddy the mongoose — had entered and likely exited through that window. He was able to establish that Colonel Barclay had not died from any blow, but from a sudden and catastrophic failure of the heart — a fit brought on by the shock of seeing Wood standing at the window. The colonel's death was, in the medical sense, entirely natural. Holmes was able to explain, furthermore, how the key came to be on the floor: Mrs. Barclay had locked the door herself earlier in the quarrel — she had locked herself and her husband in, as people sometimes do in the heat of a domestic dispute — and when she fainted she had simply dropped it where it was found. Wood had entered and departed by the window, taking Teddy with him. There was no murder.

**SMITH:** Mr. Wood — after you fled through the window that night, what were your movements? And were you not in some fear of what might follow?

**WOOD:** I was frightened, yes. I knew how it would look. I knew that I had been there, that a man was dead, and that I had run. I returned to my lodgings and remained there, not knowing what to do. When Mr. Holmes's colleague tracked me down and spoke with me, it was something of a relief, to tell you the truth. To be found. To be required to tell the truth of it, and to have a clear-minded man listen and understand. Mr. Holmes understood it perfectly. He did not judge me, which I had not expected. He simply wanted to know what had happened, and when I told him, he believed me.

**WATSON:** Holmes was quite direct with him. He made it plain that no prosecution was likely, given that no crime had been committed. Wood had entered the house uninvited, but a man cannot be charged for another man's apoplexy. The inspector — Inspector Lestrade, who was on the case — was, shall we say, less than delighted to have his theory of murder dismantled, but the medical evidence was conclusive. The coroner returned a verdict of death from natural causes, and Mrs. Barclay, who had been under something very like suspicion, was entirely cleared.

**SMITH:** Major Murphy — throughout all of this, the honor of the regiment was a matter of considerable concern to you, was it not?

**MURPHY:** It was. The regiment had been, indirectly, at the centre of a great scandal. Our colonel had died in mysterious circumstances. His wife had been suspected of his murder. And then it emerged — though Mr. Holmes was careful about how broadly he shared his findings — that the foundation of Colonel Barclay's career had been an act of treachery against a fellow soldier. You can imagine how that sat with the men. Barclay had been admired. He had been the regimental hero, in a sense — the man who had distinguished himself at Bhurtee and risen from the ranks to command. To learn that the act of distinction at Bhurtee was built upon the ruin of another man — upon a monstrous betrayal — was a very bitter thing. We held ourselves together. A regiment must. But it was a bitter thing.

**SMITH:** Mrs. Barclay — now that a considerable time has passed since these events, how do you reflect upon your husband? He was, it seems, a man capable simultaneously of great cruelty and, for many years, of domestic devotion.

**BARCLAY:** That is a question I have asked myself every day. He was not a simple man to understand. What he did to Henry Wood was — it was a wicked thing. I will not soften it. It was the act of a coward and a schemer, driven by the most selfish of motives. And yet the man I lived with, day to day, year to year — he was not without feeling. I believe he suffered for it.

The night terrors. The moods. A man who had done such a thing and felt nothing would not have lived as my husband lived — shadowed, always, by something he could not name to another soul. Whether suffering constitutes atonement — that is not for me to say. I have stopped trying to arrive at a final verdict on James Barclay. He was what he was, and I am left with what I am, and I must make what I can of it.

**SMITH:** Mr. Wood, I should like to ask you about your creature — Teddy, the mongoose. He became, in a sense, an inadvertent witness to the whole affair. Holmes made considerable use of the reports about the strange animal seen near the house that evening.

**WOOD:** Teddy is a remarkable creature. He had been my companion for a long time — longer than most friendships I have had with people, if I am honest. Mongooses are lively animals, quick and clever, and Teddy had a great affection for me and I for him. He was not responsible for the events of that evening in any way, of course. He went where I went, and when things became chaotic he followed his instincts and made his way out through the window ahead of me. The servant who saw him in the dark would not have known what manner of animal he was, and I understand why the description she gave was a confused one.

**WATSON:** Holmes identified the nature of the animal from the description with some confidence. The marks it left, the way it moved — he was able to tell that it was a creature trained or accustomed to human company. That, combined with the description of Mr. Wood himself, which matched the reports of a crooked, unusual-looking man seen in the neighborhood, allowed Holmes to form a very clear picture of the missing element in the room that night.

**SMITH:** Arthur, I want to give you an opportunity to speak to the craft of the story before we close. The title itself — "The Crooked Man" — operates on more than one level, does it not?

**DOYLE:** It does. The most obvious reading is the literal one: Henry Wood, whose body had been bent and damaged by years of captivity and mistreatment, was known locally in Aldershot as the crooked man — the strange, misshapen figure seen in the streets. But the title also reaches back toward Colonel Barclay, who was crooked in a quite different and, one might argue, far more damning sense. He had dealt crookedly —

dishonestly, treacherously — with Wood all those years ago. The man whom the world saw as straight, upright, a pillar of the regiment and a decorated officer, was in truth the more thoroughly crooked of the two. I was pleased with that double sense. It seemed to me to carry the moral of the story without stating it too bluntly. Watson's notes gave me all the raw material I needed; it was simply a question of shaping it.

**WATSON:** I should say, for the record, that Holmes himself rarely troubled himself with the moral dimensions of a case once he had solved it to his own satisfaction. He noted, with his usual detached quality, that the death of Colonel Barclay had, in a sense, saved the law considerable embarrassment, since it was not altogether clear what charge could have been laid against a man for an act of betrayal committed in wartime, three decades past. He moved on to the next problem with his usual speed. The moral weight, such as it was, he left to others.

**SMITH:** That is, perhaps, one of the qualities that makes Holmes so distinctive a figure — the perfect separation of the intellectual from the ethical, maintained with such absolute consistency. Ladies and gentlemen, we are approaching the end of our time together this afternoon, and I should like to offer each of our guests a final word. Mrs. Barclay, is there anything you would wish our audience to carry away from this story?

**BARCLAY:** Only this. People speak of buried things — buried secrets, buried guilt — as though the earth holds them safely. It does not. What is buried will surface, in the end, in one form or another. I do not say this as a warning to wrongdoers, exactly, though perhaps it serves as one. I say it as someone who lived inside a secret for many years without fully knowing it, and who found that when it finally surfaced, it surfaced all at once, and with great violence. There is no safety in concealment. There is only the interval between the concealment and the revelation.

**SMITH:** Mr. Wood?

**WOOD:** I would say only that I bear no lasting malice toward any living person in connection with these events. Colonel Barclay is gone. What was done to me cannot be undone. I am what I am, and I manage well enough. I have my creature. I have the road. There are worse lives.

**SMITH:** Major Murphy?

**MURPHY:** I would say that the Regiment endures. It has weathered this, as it has weathered other things. The men of the Royal Munsters are not defined by one man's guilt, however great that guilt may have been. I am glad the truth emerged, however painfully. A regiment, like a man, is better served by the truth than by comfortable fictions.

**SMITH:** Arthur?

**DOYLE:** I would say only that this case illustrates what Watson's notes, at their best, always illustrate: that the most extraordinary stories are not invented. They are merely found. The world is full of them, waiting for a man with the patience and the method to look properly. Holmes looked properly. That is all.

**SMITH:** And Dr. Watson?

**WATSON:** Holmes asked me once, during this very case, whether I had observed anything of interest on our journey to Aldershot. I confess I had not. He then proceeded to draw inferences from things I had seen but not remarked upon that were nothing short of astonishing. I have kept notes on a great many of his cases, and I believe I have learned, in consequence, to observe a good deal more than I once did. But I will freely admit that I have never yet caught up with him. Perhaps, in the end, that is why these seminars draw an audience: because we are all, in our way, trying to learn to observe as Holmes observes. And perhaps we never quite get there. But the attempt is worthwhile.

**SMITH:** Splendidly put, Doctor. Ladies and gentlemen, that brings our twenty-second seminar to its close. I thank our distinguished guests with all sincerity — Mrs. Nancy Barclay, Mr. Henry Wood, and Major Murphy — for their generosity in speaking with us today. I thank Arthur Conan Doyle and Dr. John H. Watson, without whom there would be no stories to celebrate and no seminars to hold. We hope to see you all again very soon. Good afternoon.

*Sustained applause*

# The Resident Patient

*First Published in August, 1893*
*Sponsored by The Strand Magazine*
*Meeting Room B, British Museum, London*

## The Twenty-Third Seminar

**Herbert Greenhough Smith** — The Strand Editor & Moderator
**Arthur Conan Doyle** — Author and Watson's Literary Agent
**Dr. John H. Watson** —Colleague and Biographer of Sherlock Holmes
**Dr. Percy Trevelyan** — Sherlock Holmes Client
**Inspector Lanner** — Scotland Yard Inspector assigned to the Case

Seminar Transcript

**SMITH:** Good afternoon, ladies and gentlemen, and welcome to the twenty-third installment of the Strand Magazine's series of public seminars commemorating the extraordinary adventures of Mr. Sherlock Holmes. I am Herbert Greenhough Smith, editor of this magazine, and it is my privilege once again to serve as your moderator. We are gathered, as always, in the splendid surroundings of the British Museum's public meeting room, and I am pleased to say that today's company is a particularly distinguished one. Joining us in our customary seats are Arthur Conan Doyle, whose pen has made these remarkable adventures available to the reading public the world over, and Dr. John H. Watson, without whose careful retention of case notes none of these narratives would be possible. Beyond our regulars, however, we have today two guests whose direct involvement in the case we are about to discuss lends the proceedings a most unusual immediacy. I refer to Dr. Percy Trevelyan, at whose Brook Street consulting rooms the events in question first came to light, and to Inspector Lanner of Scotland Yard, who was called to attend after those events reached their most alarming conclusion. Gentlemen, welcome, all of you.

**DOYLE:** Thank you, Smith. It is always a pleasure to be here, though I confess that the story we discuss today is one of the more sobering in Watson's collection. There is a darkness at the heart of "The Resident Patient" that distinguishes it from some of the more purely intellectual puzzles Holmes has been asked to solve.

**WATSON:** I should say so. When I first set down my notes from this case, I felt the weight of it rather acutely. A man was murdered under his own roof — and whatever his past, that remains a dreadful thing.

**SMITH:** Quite right, Doctor. And it is that very complexity — both of crime and of character — that makes this case so worthy of our attention today. Dr. Trevelyan, if I may, I would like to begin with you, since in many respects the case originates with your own particular circumstances at the time. Could you describe for our audience the arrangement that brought you to Brook Street?

**TREVELYAN:** With pleasure, Mr. Smith — and I must say it is rather strange to speak of it now, publicly, when I spent so much of that period uncertain whom I could trust with any part of it. But to answer your question directly: I had finished my studies and was eager to establish a practice, yet I found myself confronted with the ordinary difficulty that besets most young physicians — namely, the want of capital. I had taken my degree, and I had written what I hoped was a creditable monograph upon certain obscure nervous lesions, but ambition and attainment are not the same as funds. I had identified a practice in Brook Street that seemed most suitable for my particular interests, yet I could not secure the lease.

**SMITH:** And that is where Blessington entered the picture?

**TREVELYAN:** It is. A man came to my lodgings one evening — a stout, elderly gentleman who gave his name as Blessington. He had somehow become aware of my situation and proposed an arrangement that I confess took me by surprise in its generosity. He would defray all the expenses of the practice outright — the rent, the furnishings, the necessary equipment — and in return he would take three-quarters of my fees. Furthermore, and this was the strangest part of the arrangement, he stipulated that he himself would live in the house as a resident patient.

**WATSON:** Which struck you as unusual, I imagine.

**TREVELYAN:** It struck me as very unusual indeed. I pressed him to explain what complaint required him to live permanently in the home of a physician, and his answer was vague in the extreme. He spoke of his heart, of his nerves — nothing sufficiently definite to satisfy a medical man. But he was plainly in earnest, and the offer itself was genuinely handsome. He had a set of rooms in the upper part of the house and appeared to live comfortably enough. He paid his own way. He never interfered with my work. And so I accepted.

**DOYLE:** I should note, for the benefit of those in the audience who have read the published account, that Watson rendered the arrangement just as Dr. Trevelyan has described it. I did not embellish it in the slightest. When Watson first relayed this portion of the history to me, I remember thinking that it had rather the quality of a fairy tale — a mysterious benefactor appearing in the night. But of course, fairy tales do not always end happily.

**SMITH:** Indeed not. Dr. Trevelyan, your specialty at the time was in nervous disorders — and in catalepsy in particular, was it not?

**TREVELYAN:** Yes. As I mentioned, I had written a monograph on obscure nervous lesions, and catalepsy was among the conditions that most interested me. It is a remarkable affliction — the sudden suspension of voluntary motion, the rigidity, the insensibility — and its mechanisms were at that time, and remain to a considerable degree, imperfectly understood. I had a modest reputation in that area, modest but apparently sufficient to attract the attention of the man who came to call on me.

**SMITH:** The Russian nobleman.

**TREVELYAN:** That is what he claimed to be, yes. He was an elderly man, and he arrived at the consulting room accompanied by his son. The son, he explained, suffered from cataleptic fits of considerable severity. The father was very concerned, spoke with some difficulty in English — he had an accent that I took to be Russian — and I agreed to examine the young man. He was brought into my consulting room. The father, however, remained behind in the waiting room.

**WATSON:** That detail is critical, as Holmes was at pains to point out when you brought the matter to us.

**TREVELYAN:** Yes, though at the time I thought nothing of it. It is not unusual for a parent to wait while a patient is examined. I proceeded with my assessment of the young man's condition. He appeared to fall into a fit while I was attending to him, which naturally occupied my full attention. I was some time in the room with him. When at last the fit passed and he recovered, the two of them departed. It was only afterward, when I went upstairs, that I found Blessington in a state I had never seen in him before.

**SMITH:** Can you describe that state?

**TREVELYAN:** He was terrified. Genuinely, viscerally terrified — the pallor of his face, the trembling of his hands, the wildness in his eyes. He told me that while I had been occupied in the consulting room below, someone had entered his bedroom. He was insistent about it. He said he had come downstairs and noticed that his door was not quite as he had left it, and that certain items in his room had been disturbed. I did not dismiss his concerns, but I confess I could not see what basis there was for them. There was no sign of a forced entry, and the only strangers in the house had been the two visitors downstairs. I went to Blessington's room and examined it as carefully as I was able, but I could see nothing obviously wrong.

**WATSON:** Which is precisely why you came to Baker Street.

**TREVELYAN:** Yes. Blessington was so agitated, and so insistent that something sinister had occurred, that I felt I needed counsel from someone more qualified to read such signs than I. Holmes's name was well known to me, as to everyone in London who paid the slightest attention to the press. I went to Baker Street and laid the matter before him.

**SMITH:** Dr. Watson, I believe you were present for that consultation.

**WATSON:** I was. Holmes listened to Dr. Trevelyan's account with his customary attentiveness. He asked a number of pointed questions about the visitors — their appearance, their manner, the precise nature of the young man's fit, and, crucially, how long Trevelyan had been in the consulting room with the son while the father waited. When he had heard everything to his satisfaction, he proposed that we return with Trevelyan to Brook Street that same evening.

**SMITH:** And what did Holmes make of Blessington's room upon that visit?

**WATSON:** He found a great deal more than Trevelyan or I had been able to see. Holmes moved through that room with his characteristic methodical swiftness — the lens in hand, down on his knees at the hearth, inspecting the window, the lock, the floor. He drew our attention to certain marks in the dust, to the position of various objects, to the ash of cigars that had been smoked in the room. He identified impressions on the rug near the bed. It was plain to him that someone — more than one person, in fact — had been in that room during Trevelyan's absence, and that they had gone through it with considerable deliberation.

**TREVELYAN:** That was a most uncomfortable moment for me. I had thought Blessington overwrought, and Holmes had confirmed within a quarter of an hour that Blessington's instincts were quite correct.

**WATSON:** Holmes also spoke to Blessington directly, of course. And it was during that conversation that I noticed something I could not fully account for at the time. Blessington was not merely frightened in the way a man is frightened by a burglary — there was a specific quality to his fear, a focused dread, as though he knew perfectly well what the intrusion signified, even if he was not prepared to say so.

**SMITH:** Holmes pressed him, did he not?

**WATSON:** Holmes put some very direct questions to him. He suggested plainly that Blessington was concealing something — that whatever lay behind this affair, Blessington knew more of it than he had disclosed. Blessington denied it. He became defensive and somewhat incoherent. He gave Holmes no satisfaction, and Holmes — as I recall — remarked quite pointedly that he could not be expected to help a man who refused to help himself. We left that evening with the matter unresolved.

**SMITH:** And then came the night of the second visit.

**TREVELYAN:** Yes. Some days later, my page informed me that three men had called in the evening while I was engaged with a patient. Three men together — not the nobleman and his son as before, but three visitors at once. The boy had shown them up, apparently, but they had departed before I was free to receive them. When I heard this, I was at once uneasy and went immediately to check on Blessington.

**WATSON:** And when you went upstairs?

**TREVELYAN:** He did not answer my knock. I tried the handle. The door was not locked. I entered the room and —

**SMITH:** Take your time, Doctor.

**TREVELYAN:** Blessington was hanging from the hook on the back of the door by his own dressing gown cord. I called for help at once. Inspector Lanner was summoned from Scotland Yard.

**SMITH:** Inspector Lanner, this is the point at which you entered the matter. What were your initial impressions upon arriving at Brook Street?

**LANNER:** My first impression was that it presented all the appearances of a suicide by hanging. The body was suspended from a hook on the back of the bedroom door, the dressing gown cord was secured round the neck, and the door had not been forced. There was a chair in the vicinity that might have been used. Dr. Trevelyan, who had found the body, was in considerable distress. I secured the room, took statements, and sent for the divisional surgeon.

**SMITH:** And was it your view at first that it was, in fact, a suicide?

**LANNER:** It was consistent with that view, yes. Blessington was known to have been in a state of nervous agitation for some days prior. Dr. Trevelyan had tried on previous occasions to settle his mind. The surface of the case pointed toward a man who had worked himself into a state of despair. However — and this I will freely acknowledge — I had enough experience not to close my mind before the facts had been fully examined.

**SMITH:** Mr. Holmes was sent for again, I believe.

**WATSON:** He was. I have to say that Holmes arrived in that room and within a remarkably short time reached conclusions that materially altered the character of the entire inquiry.

**LANNER:** That is correct. I had not initially asked for Holmes, but Dr. Trevelyan had, and I was not opposed to another pair of eyes. Holmes examined the room very closely — more closely, perhaps, than any man I have seen work a scene. He paid particular attention to the cord, to the hook, to the position of the body, and to the floor and furniture.

**SMITH:** What was the result of that examination?

**WATSON:** Holmes declared without hesitation that it was murder. He had observed that the knot used to secure the cord was what he termed a 'judicial knot' — the sort employed by a professional hangman rather than by a man who has determined to end his own life in haste and distress. He observed further that the position of the body and the condition of the room were not consistent with a man who had placed himself there voluntarily. Holmes also drew attention to the ash of three separate cigars on the mantelpiece — the same evidence of multiple visitors that he had identified days before.

**LANNER:** I must say, when Holmes laid out his reasoning, it was compelling. The detail of the knot was particularly striking. I had not identified it as a judicial knot myself, but when he explained it and showed me precisely what he meant, it was not something one could reasonably dispute. Three men had been in that room — that much was supported by independent evidence as well as by Holmes's own observation — and those three men had sat in judgment on Blessington and executed sentence.

**SMITH:** That phrase — 'sat in judgment' — is a striking one. I believe Holmes eventually determined the reason for it. Dr. Watson, can you tell us what came to light regarding Blessington's true history?

**WATSON:** Holmes pieced it together from various sources. Blessington's real name was Sutton. He had been a member of a gang of criminals responsible for the robbery of the Worthington bank. The robbery itself had involved violence — a man had been shot. There were several members of the gang. When the matter came before the law, Sutton — Blessington — turned Queen's evidence against his associates. As a consequence of his testimony, one of the gang was hanged and the others were imprisoned. Blessington himself went free.

**SMITH:** And the men who came to Brook Street?

**WATSON:** Were the surviving members of that gang. They had served their sentences, been released, and had tracked Sutton down. The arrangement with Trevelyan — the comfortable rooms, the resident physician, the isolation of living in someone else's house — was

Blessington's attempt to hide himself while keeping the security of a medical man on the premises. His terror when the visitors first came was the terror of a man who recognized that he had been found.

**TREVELYAN:** That is the part that has occupied my thoughts most since the affair concluded. I had been, in a sense, engaged as part of Blessington's — Sutton's — plan for self-preservation without my knowledge or consent. He had told me nothing of any of this. His evasion of Holmes's questions, his refusal to disclose what lay behind his fear, was the refusal of a man who knew that if he explained everything, his entire carefully constructed refuge would be destroyed.

**DOYLE:** It raises a rather interesting moral question, does it not? One that I found myself turning over when Watson first gave me his notes. Blessington was a criminal who had purchased his own freedom by sending other men — his own confederates — to the gallows or to prison. Whatever one thinks of the men who killed him, the impulse behind their act was not inexplicable. Holmes himself, as Watson has recounted, held rather a measured view of the matter.

**WATSON:** He did. Holmes was thorough in his investigation, as he always is, and he was clear that murder is murder whatever the victim's history. But he did not expend a great deal of moral energy lamenting Blessington's fate. The man had made his choices and had lived for some years with their consequences pressing at the door.

**SMITH:** Inspector Lanner, how did the formal investigation proceed once Holmes's findings had altered the nature of the inquiry?

**LANNER:** Once we had accepted that Blessington's death was murder, we turned our attention to identifying and apprehending those responsible. Holmes provided us with descriptions derived from his analysis of the traces left in the room — the cigars, particularly, he had identified by type — and we worked through such records as we had. The men were identified as former members of a gang, as Dr. Watson has said. We traced their movements as best we could and determined that they had left London.

**SMITH:** And were they ultimately brought to justice?

**LANNER:** They were not brought to justice in the conventional sense, I am sorry to say. We established that they had boarded a vessel called the Norah Creina, which was bound out of British waters. That vessel was subsequently lost in a gale off the Portuguese coast. All aboard were understood to have perished. Whether that constitutes a form of justice, I leave to others to determine. From the perspective of the official investigation, the perpetrators died before they could be tried.

**SMITH:** A grim resolution.

**WATSON:** Holmes received the news with his customary equanimity. He observed, as I recall, that the matter had been taken out of human hands — which I thought a rather precise way of putting it.

**DOYLE:** I reproduced that observation, or something very close to it, in the published account. It seemed to me entirely characteristic of Holmes — that ability to acknowledge the limits of earthly justice without undue sentiment in either direction.

**SMITH:** Dr. Trevelyan, looking back at the whole affair, is there anything you would have done differently? Any moment at which the outcome might have been altered?

**TREVELYAN:** I have asked myself that question many times. I think the honest answer is that I might have pressed Blessington more urgently to speak plainly to Holmes. When Holmes told us that Blessington was concealing something, and that he could not help a man who would not help himself, I should have been more insistent with my patient. I respected his reticence because he was, in some sense, my landlord as well as my patient, and I did not wish to overreach my position. But if I had made him understand more forcefully that his safety depended upon complete candor, perhaps things might have gone differently. Perhaps not. He was a very frightened man, and frightened men do not always act rationally, even when rational action might save them.

**SMITH:** A fair and honest self-appraisal, Doctor. Inspector Lanner, is there anything in the case that you believe deserves greater recognition than the published account gives it?

**LANNER:** I would not say that the account is unfair. I would note, perhaps, that the ordinary work of the official investigation — tracing the movements of the suspected men, establishing their identities from prison records, confirming their departure from the country — is the kind of work that tends not to find its way into the more dramatic retellings. Holmes identified the meaning of the knot, Holmes identified the cigar ash, Holmes drew the picture of what had happened in that room. That is quite rightly recorded and quite rightly admired. But there is a good deal that follows from such a revelation that requires patience and the resources of Scotland Yard, and it is the combination of the two that constitutes a proper inquiry.

**WATSON:** A point well taken, and one that I hope I have not done too poor a job of acknowledging in my account. Holmes himself was always careful to say that he could not have functioned without the official machinery of the law, however much he might occasionally comment upon its shortcomings.

**SMITH:** Mr. Doyle, I have a question for you that I have been saving for this point in our conversation. In writing this story for publication in the Strand, were there any aspects of Watson's original notes that you found particularly challenging to render for the reading public?

**DOYLE:** The challenge, as ever, was one of compression and shape. Watson's notes are thorough, but a case of this kind has rather a complex architecture — there is the seemingly mundane arrangement between Trevelyan and Blessington, there is the visit of the Russian nobleman and his son, there is Blessington's terror, there is the murder and Holmes's analysis of it, and then there is the revelation of the historical crime that underlies everything. To move the reader from one phase to the next without losing the thread requires a certain care. I was particularly attentive to the pacing of Blessington's revelation — or rather, the revelations about him, since he himself never disclosed the truth — because the reader's understanding of who Blessington really was must arrive at the right moment to give the tragedy its proper weight.

**SMITH:** You refer to him as a tragic figure.

**DOYLE:** In a qualified sense, yes. He was a man who had betrayed his associates to save himself, and who then spent years attempting to feel safe in a world that was always liable to catch up with him. The rooms in Brook Street, the comfortable arrangement with Dr. Trevelyan, the careful seclusion — all of it was the picture of a man who lived in fear. That is not entirely without its pathetic dimension, even if one cannot feel sympathy for someone whose betrayal sent another man to the gallows.

**WATSON:** I confess I struggle with it. As a medical man, I am trained to consider my patient's welfare without reference to their moral history. Blessington was my patient, in a sense, by virtue of my accompanying Holmes to his rooms and examining him. He was not well — not well in his nerves, in his heart. And he was a man who ended his days in a noose, alone in a room in the small hours, with none of those he might have called friends aware of what was happening to him.

**TREVELYAN:** I was in the house that night. That is the fact I cannot quite lay aside. I was in the house, and I did not hear anything. I do not know what I could have done differently — three determined men are not to be stopped by a single physician — but I was there, and it happened, and that is not easily forgotten.

**SMITH:** Thank you for that honesty, Dr. Trevelyan. Gentlemen, we are coming toward the end of our time together, and I wonder if each of you might offer a final thought on what this case represents in the broader context of Holmes's career. Dr. Watson?

**WATSON:** It represents, I think, the limits of what Holmes's methods can achieve when a central witness refuses to cooperate. Holmes saw clearly that Blessington held information essential to his own rescue, and Blessington would not give it. There is no analysis, however brilliant, that can substitute for the willingness of those involved to act on good advice. Holmes was right about the danger. He was right about the cover-up. He was right about the murder. But he was not able to prevent it, and that fact mattered to him, I believe, though he did not dwell upon it.

**TREVELYAN:** For me it is a case that permanently altered my understanding of how little we may know of those closest to us in daily life. Blessington lived under my roof for years. I examined him, I spoke with him, I dined with him on occasion. And I knew almost nothing of his real history, his real name, or the terror in which he spent his waking hours.

**LANNER:** From the professional standpoint, I would say that it is a case which demonstrates the value of not forming a conclusion before the evidence has been fully gathered. The appearance of suicide was plausible.

Had we acted upon appearance rather than investigation, three murderers would have gone entirely unchallenged, and whatever rough justice the sea provided would have been the only accounting for Blessington's death. The work of investigation — slow and unglamorous as it often is — matters.

**DOYLE:** My own final thought is one of craft, perhaps inevitably. This is a story that contains, at its core, an older story — the Worthington bank robbery, the trial, the betrayal — which the reader never sees directly but which casts its shadow over everything. Writing that kind of case requires trust in the reader's imagination. I did not need to describe the robbery itself; I needed only to make clear that it had happened, and that it had consequences that time had not dissolved. Holmes's genius, and Watson's skill in recording it, is at its most interesting to me when the puzzle has that layered quality — when the present crime cannot be understood without understanding the past.

**SMITH:** Beautifully put, Arthur. And on that note, ladies and gentlemen, I believe we must bring our twenty-third seminar to a close. I thank Dr. Percy Trevelyan and Inspector Lanner for lending their firsthand experience to our proceedings today — your candor and your patience in answering our questions have enriched our understanding of this case immeasurably. I thank, as always, Arthur Conan Doyle and Dr. John H. Watson, without whom none of these evenings would be possible. And I thank our audience here at the British Museum for their attentive company. Good evening to you all.

*Sustained applause*

# The Greek Interpreter

*First Published in September, 1893*
*Sponsored by The Strand Magazine*
*Meeting Room B, British Museum, London*

**The Twenty-Fourth Seminar**

**Herbert Greenhough Smith** — The Strand Editor & Moderator
**Arthur Conan Doyle** — Author and Watson's Literary Agent
**Dr. John H. Watson** —Colleague and Biographer of Sherlock Holmes
**Mr. Melas** — The Greek Interpreter
**Inspector Gregson** — Scotland Yard Inspector assigned to the Case

Seminar Transcript

**SMITH:** Good afternoon, ladies and gentlemen, and welcome once again to our ongoing series of commemorative seminars celebrating the singular adventures of Mr. Sherlock Holmes, as they have appeared in the pages of The Strand Magazine. I am Herbert Greenhough Smith, editor of the Strand, and I am deeply honored to serve, as always, as your moderator. This is our twenty-fourth gathering in the series, and I am pleased to report that enthusiasm among our readers and among the general public shows no sign of abating. Today we turn our attention to a story which is, in my estimation, one of the most remarkable in the entire canon — not only for the drama of its events, but for what it reveals about the extraordinary Holmes family, of which most of the world had been entirely ignorant until this tale was set before them. We are here to discuss "The Adventure of the Greek Interpreter." Joining us today, as ever, are Arthur Conan Doyle, without whose skill and labor these stories would never have reached the reading public, and Dr. John H. Watson, who provided the case notes from which Arthur worked. In addition, we are honored this afternoon by the presence of two gentlemen whose roles in the affair were direct and, in one instance, deeply harrowing. I refer to Mr. Melas, a Greek interpreter residing in Pall Mall, and to Inspector Tobias Gregson of Scotland Yard. Gentlemen, on behalf of the Strand Magazine and this audience, I thank you for being here.

*Applause from the audience.*

**DOYLE:** Thank you, Mr. Smith. It is always a pleasure.

**WATSON:** Indeed. Though I confess that certain of these seminars bring back memories more comfortable than others. Today's story falls rather firmly in the second category, at least as far as poor Mr. Melas is concerned.

**MELAS:** You are very kind to say so, Dr. Watson. I will acknowledge freely that the memory of those events is not one I revisit without a shudder. But I am glad to be here, and glad that the affair, in the end, was not worse than it was — though it was bad enough.

**GREGSON:** I echo that. It was a strange and troubling business from beginning to end. Not the sort of case that sits easily in the mind.

**SMITH:** Let us begin, then, at the beginning — or rather, at what the readers of the Strand encountered at the beginning. Dr. Watson, this story is notable for something that precedes the case itself — the revelation that Mr. Sherlock Holmes has a brother. How did that come about?

**WATSON:** It came about in the most natural fashion, though I confess the revelation startled me considerably. Holmes and I had been passing an evening together, and he had been, as was his habit from time to time, demonstrating his powers of observation upon my own person. I had made some remark about his singular gifts, and he replied quite calmly that in point of fact he had a brother who possessed greater powers of observation than he himself. I did not believe it at first. I am not certain I believed it until I had actually met Mr. Mycroft Holmes.

**DOYLE:** And that meeting, as it happened, occurred almost immediately thereafter, because it was Mycroft who brought the plight of Mr. Melas to Sherlock's attention.

**SMITH:** Exactly. Mr. Melas, before we discuss your ordeal in detail, could you tell us something about how you came to know Mycroft Holmes in the first place?

**MELAS:** Certainly. I reside in Pall Mall, and for some years I had been acquainted by proximity and occasional encounter with Mr. Mycroft Holmes, who is also a resident of that street. He is a man of such commanding presence and such piercing intelligence that one could not help but take note of him, even if one's contact was no more than a nodding acquaintance. We had spoken on a number of occasions, though always briefly. He knew my profession — that of a Greek interpreter, which I had practiced for many years in London. It was natural enough, then, that when I found myself in desperate need of assistance and had managed to return home, I went first to Mr. Mycroft Holmes.

**SMITH:** And he brought the matter to his brother Sherlock without delay?

**MELAS:** He did, that very evening. I am convinced that but for the speed with which Mr. Mycroft acted, I would not be sitting here before you today.

**SMITH:** Let us walk through the events as they unfolded. Mr. Melas, you were approached by a man named Harold Latimer with a proposal of employment. Can you describe that approach and what followed?

**MELAS:** I can. It was an evening when I had returned home late, having been engaged upon other professional business. A fellow was waiting for me — a man who gave his name as Harold Latimer. He was a large, coarse-featured man, powerfully built, and there was something about him that I instinctively mistrusted, though I could not immediately say why. He told me he required the services of an interpreter and was willing to pay very handsomely. I was to accompany him that very night.

**WATSON:** And you agreed?

**MELAS:** I agreed, somewhat against my better judgment. He was persuasive, and the sum he mentioned was considerable. We took a carriage — a four-wheeled cab — and it was here that my misgivings deepened sharply. The windows of the cab were covered, so that I could not see where we were going. I attempted to observe what I could through any small gap available to me, and I concluded at various points that we had crossed the Thames and that we had travelled a considerable distance, but beyond that I could determine little. The journey lasted well over an hour.

**DOYLE:** In the story I rendered it as Holmes and Watson making subsequent deductions about the route and the probable location of the house, based upon the time and direction of travel as Mr. Melas had described them.

**WATSON:** Yes, Holmes was quite precise about it. He reasoned from Mr. Melas's account of the direction in which they had driven, the time elapsed, and other details, and concluded that the house was likely south of the Thames, and at a considerable remove from the centre of London.

**SMITH:** Mr. Melas, when you arrived at this house, what did you find?

**MELAS:** I was brought into a large, poorly lit room. There was a man seated at a table across from me — and I must say that the sight of him was deeply alarming. He was thin, very thin, with the look of a man who had not been properly fed for some time. His face was pale and drawn. He was, as I learned through the conversation that followed, a Greek. His name — which I was not permitted to speak openly, but which I eventually discerned — was Mr. Paul Kratides. He had come, I understood, from Athens.

**SMITH:** And there was sticking plaster used upon him at some point, was there not?

**MELAS:** There was, yes. When I first saw him, the sticking plaster had been affixed across his lips to prevent him from speaking freely. It was a barbarous thing. When it was removed for purposes of the conversation I was expected to facilitate, I could see what it had concealed — a man in great distress, physically weakened, desperate to communicate something but constrained at every turn.

**WATSON:** Holmes was particularly struck by that detail when you described it. The deliberate use of plaster to prevent speech struck him as evidence of a cold and calculating cruelty.

**SMITH:** What was the nature of the questions you were instructed to put to this man?

**MELAS:** The questions all centered upon a single object — the signing of papers. I was told to ask Mr. Kratides whether he was prepared to sign documents that had been placed before him. The implication, though it was never stated in so many words, was that these documents concerned property. Mr. Kratides refused, repeatedly and firmly, despite being clearly in a condition of great physical weakness.

**SMITH:** And the other man present — the associate of Latimer?

**MELAS:** That was Wilson Kemp. A thin, sandy-haired man with a weak chin and a cold, watchful manner. He said very little during the interview, but his presence was menacing. It was clear that he and Latimer were acting in concert.

**DOYLE:** I should note, for those in the audience who have read the story, that Kemp's name is given in the published version, though Mr. Melas had to piece it together gradually from what he could observe.

**SMITH:** Mr. Melas, you did something rather extraordinary during this interview. While ostensibly serving as interpreter, you were conducting a private communication with Mr. Kratides. How did you manage that?

**MELAS:** It required some care. The questions I was given to translate were simple enough, and I translated them faithfully so far as Latimer was concerned — he knew no Greek whatever, which was of course why I had been brought there. But I inserted, within my translations, additional questions of my own. I asked Mr. Kratides who he was, how long he had been in that place, and whether there was a woman involved. He was able to answer these within his replies, and I was able to extract the information before rendering his responses back to Latimer in English.

**WATSON:** A remarkable piece of quick thinking under pressure.

**MELAS:** Necessity sharpens the mind, Dr. Watson. I knew that I was in a dangerous situation, that the man before me was in an even more dangerous one, and that whatever I could learn might later be of use. I learned that there was indeed a woman — a Miss Sophy Kratides — and that she was Paul Kratides's sister. The implication, from what I could gather, was that she was also being held in that house.

**SMITH:** Inspector Gregson, when did Scotland Yard enter the picture?

**GREGSON:** Not as early as I should have liked, Mr. Smith. The matter was brought to us by Mr. Sherlock Holmes, who had by that point made his own inquiries. I will be candid: Holmes came to us with specific information about the likely location of the house in question, and we acted upon it. The investigation benefited considerably from the work he had already done.

**WATSON:** Holmes had placed an advertisement in the newspapers — I believe several of the evening papers — on the theory that if Mr. Melas saw it, he would respond, and if he did not respond, that silence would itself be informative.

**MELAS:** I did not see it, as it happened. I had already gone back to that house.

**SMITH:** You had been summoned a second time?

**MELAS:** I had. Once again I was collected in the evening, once again the carriage windows were obscured, and once again I was taken to the same house. But the second visit was very different in character. There was a sense of great urgency about it, almost of panic, on the part of Latimer and Kemp. The questions were more pressing, the atmosphere more threatening. And then the interview was terminated abruptly. I was taken away from the room, and shortly thereafter I was not fully conscious of what was happening to me.

**WATSON:** When we arrived at the house, we found both Mr. Melas and Mr. Kratides unconscious from the fumes of a charcoal fire that had been left burning in the room where they were confined. The windows had been sealed.

*A murmur from the audience*

**GREGSON:** It was fortunate beyond measure that we arrived when we did. A matter of another hour and I do not think we should have found either of them alive. As it was, Mr. Kratides was in a very grave condition.

**MELAS:** I owe my life to the speed with which Mr. Holmes and Dr. Watson and Inspector Gregson acted that night. I have never forgotten that, and I never shall.

**SMITH:** Arthur, you have written of Holmes's methods throughout this series of adventures. In this story, there is a particular emphasis on the chain of reasoning by which he located the house. Would you describe that for us?

**DOYLE:** Certainly. When Holmes heard Mr. Melas's account of the first visit — the blindfolded carriage journey, the general direction, the time elapsed — he began to narrow the field of possible locations. The details of the house itself as Mr. Melas described it, together with the knowledge that a party of three foreigners had lately taken up residence south of London, allowed Holmes to make his inquiry. It is characteristic of Holmes that he did not merely reason upon what he had been told, but went and collected additional information before he was satisfied that he knew where to go. The urgency of the matter — the recognition that a man was being held against his will and was possibly in grave danger — meant that there was no leisure for drawn-out investigation.

**WATSON:** Holmes also perceived, from the advertised notice that Mycroft had seen, the underlying design of the whole affair. Latimer and Kemp wished Mr. Kratides to sign papers — the precise nature of which was not made entirely plain — and they were holding him and his sister in order to compel that signature. The sister, Miss Sophy Kratides, was the instrument of leverage.

**SMITH:** And yet, despite all their efforts, Mr. Kratides never did sign those papers?

**MELAS:** He did not. Whatever else may be said of him, Paul Kratides was a man of considerable courage. He had been starved, imprisoned, threatened — and he refused to yield. I admired him greatly, though our acquaintance was confined to those strange whispered exchanges during the interview.

**SMITH:** Inspector Gregson, when the party arrived at the house, what was the scene?

**GREGSON:** The house appeared outwardly quiet. There was no sign of Latimer or Kemp — they had already fled. We gained entry and made our way through the rooms. It was in one of the lower rooms that we found the two men. The charcoal fumes were thick and the atmosphere nearly unbreathable. We removed Mr. Melas and Mr. Kratides at once and did what could be done for them. Dr. Watson was present and rendered immediate assistance.

**WATSON:** Mr. Kratides had been in that weakened state for some considerable time before the fumes were introduced. His constitution could not withstand it. He died without recovering consciousness. Mr. Melas, owing to his generally stronger condition, survived.

**MELAS:** I remember very little of that night after I was taken from the room in which we had been confined. My next clear memory is of waking in much better surroundings and being told what had happened. The news that Mr. Kratides had not survived was deeply painful to me. We had managed only a few words between us, but he had struck me as a man of genuine worth.

**SMITH:** And Latimer and Kemp — they escaped entirely?

**GREGSON:** From England, yes. They were gone before we arrived. I will not pretend that was a satisfactory outcome from the Yard's point of view. Inquiries were made through the proper channels on the Continent, but the two men had vanished into Europe and we had no immediate intelligence of their whereabouts.

**WATSON:** Holmes received a communication about them some time afterward — a cutting from a foreign newspaper, if I recall correctly.

**DOYLE:** Yes. The cutting reported that two Englishmen matching the descriptions of Latimer and Kemp had been found dead under violent circumstances in Hungary — or was it in the Balkans? The circumstances suggested that they had been killed by a woman.

**WATSON:** The implication was clear. Miss Sophy Kratides had found them.

*A moment of quiet in the room*

**SMITH:** That is a striking end to the affair. Arthur, you presented it in the story without elaboration — simply the news item, with its grim implication. Was that a deliberate choice?

**DOYLE:** It was. There are moments when understatement serves better than explanation. The reader understands perfectly well what has happened. Sophy Kratides had lost her brother through the actions of these two men. What followed required no commentary from me.

**WATSON:** Holmes, when I showed him the cutting, remarked upon it in his typically detached fashion. He observed that it had come to a natural end, or words to that effect. He was not given to lengthy moral pronouncements.

**SMITH:** Mr. Melas, I want to return to the advertisement that Dr. Watson mentioned — the one placed in the papers. You said you did not see it. How did you come to learn of it afterward, and what was your reaction?

**MELAS:** I learned of it when I was told the full account of how I had been found. The advertisement, as I understood it, was intended to alert me that someone was aware of my predicament and was seeking information. Holmes and Watson and Mr. Mycroft Holmes had put the notice in several of the evening papers in the hope that either I would read it and respond, or that no response would confirm that I was still in the hands of Latimer and Kemp. My reaction, when I heard of it, was one of profound gratitude. That anyone had thought so clearly and acted so quickly on what must have seemed incomplete and confusing information really surprised me.

**SMITH:** Dr. Watson, this story marks the first appearance of Mycroft Holmes in the pages of the Strand. You have described him as possessing even greater powers of observation and deduction than his brother. Do you stand by that assessment?

**WATSON:** It is not so much my own assessment as Holmes's. He said it himself. He told me that Mycroft had faculties of observation and deduction that exceeded his own, but that Mycroft lacked the energy and the ambition to put those faculties into practical use. Sherlock seeks a conclusion and pursues it wherever it leads. Mycroft is content — or so I understood Holmes to mean — to sit in his armchair and to think. The Diogenes Club, where Mycroft was a member, seemed to me perfectly suited to that temperament.

**SMITH:** You visited the Diogenes Club in connection with this case?

**WATSON:** We did. Holmes brought me there to meet Mycroft and to hear his account of Mr. Melas's situation firsthand. The Club is an extraordinary institution — one of the most peculiar I have ever entered. Its rules forbid any talking in the common rooms, the members being, as Holmes described them, the most unsociable and unclubable men in London. There is a single room — the Strangers' Room — where conversation is permitted. It was there that we sat with Mycroft and heard what he had to say.

**DOYLE:** I must confess that the Diogenes Club gave me great pleasure to invent. There is something wonderfully comic and yet somehow believable about a club whose defining characteristic is the absolute refusal to acknowledge the existence of other members.

*Laughter from the audience*

**GREGSON:** I have met men who would find such a club entirely congenial. Certain of my colleagues at the Yard, for instance.

*More laughter*

**SMITH:** Arthur, I should like to ask about the challenge this story presented to you as a writer. The mechanics of the deception — the secret communication embedded in the interpreter's translations — required that the reader follow a conversation that is happening on two levels simultaneously. How did you approach that?

**DOYLE:** It was one of the more technically demanding passages in the whole series. The problem was to make it clear to the reader that Melas was asking questions within his translations that Latimer could not hear or understand, while at the same time conveying the texture of a real conversation — the pressure, the menace, the desperation on all sides. I relied upon Dr. Watson's notes, which were quite detailed on this point, and I tried to render the exchange as simply and directly as possible without robbing it of its dramatic tension.

**MELAS:** I had set down an account of the exchange as accurately as I could remember it, almost immediately after returning home from the first visit. Memory, when the mind has been keenly engaged, can be remarkably precise. I was able to reconstruct most of the conversation quite fully.

**WATSON:** Holmes was struck by that written account. He asked Melas a great many questions about the precise wording of various exchanges. He was particularly interested in what Kratides had been able to convey about how long he had been held, and about the woman.

**SMITH:** And the woman — Miss Sophy Kratides. She is a figure who appears in the story largely as an absence, and yet she casts a very long shadow over events, both in the main narrative and in that final newspaper cutting. Mr. Melas, did you have any direct contact with her?

**MELAS:** No direct contact. During the first visit, I became aware that there was a woman somewhere in the house — the brother's agitation when I touched upon the subject made that clear enough. But I did not see her. I cannot tell you what she looked like or say anything of her character beyond what may be inferred from how the story concluded.

**WATSON:** Holmes speculated about her at some length after the fact, though he never met her either, to my knowledge. He surmised that she was a woman of considerable resolution — that the hold which Latimer and Kemp had over her brother was the mechanism by which they sought to bend her to their will, and that when that mechanism had served its dreadful purpose, she had been free to act as she saw fit.

**DOYLE:** The story, as I say, requires no commentary on that point. It speaks for itself.

**SMITH:** Inspector Gregson, I want to give you the opportunity to speak to the broader question of jurisdiction and cooperation. This case involved a foreign national, events that had begun overseas, and criminals who fled to the Continent. From the Yard's perspective, what were the particular difficulties?

**GREGSON:** The particular difficulty was the speed of it all. From the time we received actionable information to the time we arrived at the house, the window was very narrow. Latimer and Kemp were, in retrospect, already making their preparations to leave. We arrived too late to apprehend them, but in time — just barely in time — to prevent a worse outcome for Mr. Melas. As to the international dimension, the Yard is accustomed to working through official channels with our counterparts on the Continent, but those channels are slow, and men who are determined to disappear can do so more easily than we should like.

**WATSON:** Holmes was of the view, I think, that Latimer and Kemp had always intended to depart England once their objective was achieved — or once it became clear that it could not be achieved.

**GREGSON:** Very likely. The whole operation had about it the character of a smash-and-grab, if you will forgive the expression. They had come to this country for a specific purpose, with a specific person in mind, and they were prepared to move quickly.

**SMITH:** Mr. Melas, this is perhaps an indelicate question, but — was there ever a moment, during either of those visits, when you considered simply doing as you were told and saying nothing of the private communications you were conducting with Mr. Kratides?

**MELAS:** That is not an indelicate question at all. It is the most natural question in the world, and I would be dishonest if I claimed there was no temptation. I was frightened. There were moments of very sharp fear. These were not gentle men — they made that clear through manner and implication even before any direct threat was offered. But I am an interpreter by profession and by nature, Mr. Smith. My whole vocation depends upon the faithful transmission of meaning between people who cannot otherwise communicate. There was a man before me who was imprisoned and suffering and who needed to tell someone what had happened to him. I could not simply look away from that.

*Sustained applause from the audience*

**WATSON:** Holmes, when he heard that account, said — and I record this because I thought it worth preserving — that Mr. Melas had shown more practical courage than many a man who had been decorated for it.

**MELAS:** You are very generous, and so was Mr. Holmes. I think, in truth, that I acted partly on instinct and partly out of the simple professional habit of doing one's job properly, even under duress.

**SMITH:** Dr. Watson, you narrate this story in the first person, as you do the others. But you were not present at the initial conversation between

Holmes and Mycroft, nor during the events at the house in the way that Mr. Melas was. How did you assemble the narrative?

**WATSON:** I was present for more than might appear from the page. I accompanied Holmes to the Diogenes Club and heard Mycroft's account directly. I was in the carriage with Holmes when we drove to the house. I was there when we found Mr. Melas and Mr. Kratides. The portions of the narrative that preceded Holmes's involvement — Mr. Melas's account of his two visits — I took down from Mr. Melas himself, partly that same night and partly in subsequent conversation. He proved a very exact and reliable witness.

**MELAS:** Dr. Watson asked excellent questions. He helped me to remember details that I might otherwise have let slip from my account — the smell of the house, the quality of the light, small things of that sort that turned out to matter.

**SMITH:** Arthur, a final question for you, and then I shall invite our guests to offer any closing thoughts. Looking back at this story now, what strikes you most about it?

**DOYLE:** What strikes me most, I think, is the family portrait — unexpected and quietly significant. Holmes had never mentioned Mycroft to Watson. Watson had assumed Holmes to be, in some fundamental sense, alone in the world — a man without the ordinary ties of family and background. The revelation that there was a brother, and a brother of such remarkable quality, changed the picture considerably. It reminded me — and perhaps reminded readers — that Sherlock Holmes, for all his singular qualities, had not sprung fully formed from nowhere. He came from somewhere. He had blood relations. He was, in some sense that the stories do not often dwell upon, a man.

**WATSON:** I found Mycroft a deeply interesting figure then, and I find him so still. He and Sherlock are alike in their gifts and utterly unlike in their habits and dispositions. There is a quality in Mycroft — a monumental stillness, a preference for thought over action — that I have never seen in anyone else.

**SMITH:** Mr. Melas, a closing word?

**MELAS:** Only that I am grateful — to Mr. Sherlock Holmes and his brother, to Dr. Watson, to Inspector Gregson, and to everyone who acted that night with the speed and judgment that saved my life. I am grateful also for the opportunity to speak here today. Paul Kratides cannot speak for himself. I am glad that the story of what was done to him — and what he refused to yield to — has been told, and told as well as Arthur has told it.

**GREGSON:** I would add only this: the case reminded me, as a number of my encounters with Holmes have done, that there are forms of investigation and reasoning that lie beyond what the ordinary resources of a police force can accomplish in the time available. That is not a comfortable admission for a man of my position, but it is an honest one.

**SMITH:** And on that admirably candid note, I think we must bring this session to a close. Ladies and gentlemen, on behalf of the Strand Magazine, I thank our guests — Arthur Conan Doyle, Dr. John Watson, Mr. Melas, and Inspector Tobias Gregson — and I thank this audience for its attention and its enthusiasm. Good afternoon.

*Applause. The participants remain at the table as audience members approach*

# The Naval Treaty

*First Published in October-November, 1893*
*Sponsored by The Strand Magazine*
*Meeting Room B, British Museum, London*

## The Twenty-Fifth Seminar

**Herbert Greenhough Smith** — The Strand Editor & Moderator
**Arthur Conan Doyle** — Author and Watson's Literary Agent
**Dr. John H. Watson** —Colleague and Biographer of Sherlock Holmes
**Mr. Percy Phelps** — Entrusted to copy the Naval Treaty
**Miss Annie Harrison** — Engaged to be Married to Percy Phelps
**Inspector Forbes** — Scotland Yard Inspector assigned to the Case

### Seminar Transcript

**SMITH:** Ladies and gentlemen, welcome to the twenty-fifth in our series of seminars here at the British Museum, produced under the auspices of *The Strand Magazine.* Today, we turn to what many of our readers have described as one of the most gripping narratives in the entire canon — the case known as "The Naval Treaty." I am Herbert Greenhough Smith, your moderator. With me tonight, as always, is the author of the published account, Arthur Conan Doyle, and the gentleman whose own case notes form the foundation of everything Arthur sets down, Dr. John H. Watson. We are further honored by the presence of three individuals whose roles in this remarkable affair were quite central: Mr. Percy Phelps, who was at the very heart of the crisis; Miss Annie Harrison, who provided Mr. Phelps with care and shelter during his long illness; and Inspector Forbes of Scotland Yard, who led the official investigation. Welcome to you all.

**DOYLE:** Thank you, Mr. Smith. I am very glad to have Percy, Miss Harrison, and Inspector Forbes here. I confess that when Watson first laid this case before me I felt the weight of it immediately — the disappearance of a document with such enormous consequences for England's position in Europe, the long weeks of illness, and then the remarkable intervention of Holmes. It has all the elements that make these narratives live.

**WATSON:** I should perhaps begin by explaining how I came to know Mr. Phelps at all, for it sets the scene. Percy and I were at school together, and though we had not met for years, when his letter reached me I felt at once the urgency behind it. He described his situation in terms that no old friend could disregard.

**PHELPS:** I am grateful you came, Watson — both then and now. I hardly knew what I was writing in those days. Nine weeks had passed since the night of the catastrophe, and I was, I think, not entirely myself. The thought that the treaty was still missing, that I had failed my uncle, that my career and reputation lay in ruins — it weighed upon me with a force that is difficult to convey to anyone who has not experienced it.

**SMITH:** Mr. Phelps, let us go back to that evening — the night the treaty vanished. You had been entrusted by your uncle, Lord Holdhurst, the Foreign Minister, with copying out this document. Can you describe the circumstances?

**PHELPS:** Yes. My uncle had placed considerable confidence in me by giving me the task at all. It was a treaty of some delicacy — an agreement between England and Italy, the terms of which, if they had become known at that time to the French or Russian governments, might have had very serious consequences. Lord Holdhurst wished to avoid involving more clerks than absolutely necessary, and so I undertook to copy the document myself, working late in the evening when the office was quiet. I was alone in the room — my colleague, Mr. Charles Gorot, had gone home — and I set to work. It was somewhere near ten o'clock when I felt the need of some coffee. A commissionaire remains all night in a little lodge at the foot of the stairs, and is in the habit of making coffee at his spirit-lamp for any of the officials who may be working overtime. I rang the bell, therefore, to summon him. To my surprise, it was a woman who answered the summons, a large, coarse-faced, elderly woman, in an apron. She explained that she was the commissionaire's wife, and I gave her the order for the coffee. It seemed to take a long time for the coffee to arrive, so I went downstairs to see for myself what was taking so long. I found the commissionaire fast asleep in his box, with the kettle boiling furiously upon the spirit-lamp, for the water was spurting over the floor. I had put out my hand and was about to shake the man, who was still sleeping soundly, when a bell over his head rang loudly.

**SMITH:** The bell rang?

**PHELPS:** Yes — a bell rang in the corridor, indicating that someone was at the door of the office. I thought nothing of it particularly; I went out to answer it, but found no one. When I returned — it could not have been more than a minute or two — the treaty was gone from the table where I had left it. Gone. I searched everywhere. There was simply no explanation that presented itself to my mind. I was alone; the commissionaire had not yet returned; and the document had vanished.

**WATSON:** I remember, when you described it to us at Briarbrae, the helpless bewilderment in your face. You said yourself that you could make nothing of it.

**PHELPS:** Nothing whatsoever. And the worst of it was that I could tell no one the full truth without revealing the nature of what had been taken. My uncle had impressed upon me the necessity of secrecy. The treaty itself was never to be spoken of outside the Foreign Office.

**SMITH:** Inspector Forbes, at what point did Scotland Yard become involved?

**FORBES:** Very promptly, Mr. Smith. A matter of this nature — a document of State significance disappearing from a government office — was not the kind of thing that could be left to chance. I was called in without delay and began my inquiries. I questioned Mr. Phelps, I examined the room, and I turned my attention to those who had been in or near the premises that evening. The commissionaire Tangey was a natural subject of interest, and I also looked closely at his wife, who had been present that night to bring him his supper.

**SMITH:** What did you make of Tangey and his wife?

**FORBES:** Tangey himself seemed a straightforward man with a clean record. His wife was another matter — her behaviour struck me as suspicious when she was questioned, and we watched her movements carefully. I will not say my suspicions were wholly unreasonable. But in the end, nothing conclusive came from that line of inquiry. The treaty did not pass through the hands of either of them, as events eventually proved.

**WATSON:** I recall that when Holmes and I came down to Woking to see Percy, Holmes asked specifically about Tangey's wife — whether she had been examined, what her manner had been. Inspector Forbes, you and Holmes were not, I think, entirely in step with one another from the outset.

**FORBES:** I will be candid, Doctor. I had — and I still have — a good deal of respect for Mr. Holmes's abilities. But it is not always comfortable to have a private individual pursuing the same investigation as Scotland Yard, and I confess I felt that we were quite capable of managing the matter without assistance. I told Holmes as much. I said that I had every ground that he had, and that I was capable of drawing my own conclusions. That is my honest recollection.

**DOYLE:** And yet Holmes saw something that the official investigation had not fastened upon?

**FORBES:** Eventually, yes. I will not pretend otherwise. The resolution of the case belonged to Holmes, and I am honest enough to acknowledge it. He followed a thread that I had not given sufficient weight to. The question of who, beyond Mr. Phelps himself, had had any awareness of the treaty or the circumstances of that evening — that, it turned out, was the key.

**SMITH:** Miss Harrison, you were at Briarbrae throughout the period of Mr. Phelps's illness. Can you tell us something of those weeks?

**ANNIE:** Percy was very ill. The shock of that night — the sudden collapse of everything he had worked for, the fear that he had been made to seem a thief or a traitor — it was more than his nerves could withstand. He came to Briarbrae because there was nowhere else for him to go, and because I wanted very much to look after him. My brother Joseph was good enough to take us both in. For nine weeks Percy lay in the little room at the corner of the house, and I nursed him as best I could. There were days when I feared he would never fully recover.

**WATSON:** I found him greatly changed from the Percy Phelps I remembered at school — pale and wasted, though the keenness of his mind was still there when he was roused by the subject of the treaty. He could not leave it alone, even in his illness.

**PHELPS:** How could I? Every waking hour it was with me. The knowledge that somewhere the document existed — that it might already have found its way into foreign hands — that I was responsible. I could not rest.

**SMITH:** Mr. Phelps, when Dr. Watson arrived at Briarbrae with Mr. Holmes, what was your first impression of Holmes?

**PHELPS:** That he was remarkably alert. The moment he arrived, I felt — and I say this without any disrespect to Inspector Forbes, who had worked diligently — that something different was about to happen. Holmes examined everything with a thoroughness that was almost startling. He had questions that I had never been asked, and he seemed particularly interested in what I could tell him about the night itself — the exact sequence of events, the ring of the bell, the time Tangey had been gone, how long I was away from the table when I went to the door. He gave the impression of a man constructing something in his mind, block by block.

**WATSON:** Holmes also visited the Foreign Office itself, as I recall. He went up to London the following day and inspected the room where the document had been copied.

**PHELPS:** Yes. And he met with my uncle, Lord Holdhurst. I understand Lord Holdhurst was quite open with him — more open, I believe, than he had been with anyone else. Holmes seemed to inspire a confidence that was difficult to resist.

**SMITH:** Inspector Forbes, did you feel at any stage that Holmes was interfering with your investigation, or crowding your inquiries?

**FORBES:** Crowding is perhaps too strong a word. But when a private detective is pursuing the same case as Scotland Yard, there is inevitably some friction. Holmes was not discourteous — I will give him that. But he had a way of suggesting, by manner alone, that he had already moved beyond the point at which official inquiry had stalled. I found that slightly irritating at the time, though in retrospect I understand it better. He was, in the end, correct.

**DOYLE:** Watson's account conveys that well, I think. Holmes had the capacity to see where others had stopped — to ask whether a conclusion that seemed settled was in fact settled at all. In this case, the circle of inquiry had fixed itself too narrowly, and he was able to widen it.

**SMITH:** Let us turn to what I think many in this room will consider the most singular portion of the entire affair — the evening on which Holmes set his trap at Briarbrae. Watson, Holmes gave you and Mr. Phelps some rather unusual instructions, did he not?

**WATSON:** He did, and I confess they puzzled me considerably at the time. Holmes told Percy and me to go up to London — to leave Briarbrae entirely. He was quite firm about it. He said he wished us out of the way for the evening, and that we were to make no fuss about the matter. Percy was reluctant, naturally — the house was his refuge, and the idea of being sent away from it seemed strange to him. But Holmes has a manner, when he is resolved upon something, that does not invite argument. We went.

**PHELPS:** I remember feeling rather helpless about it. Holmes had given me no explanation — simply the instruction that Watson and I were to take ourselves to London. I trusted him, of course, or tried to. But sitting in a train carriage while someone else managed the crisis in your own house is a peculiarly unsettling experience.

**SMITH:** Miss Harrison, before Holmes sent Percy and Watson away, he gave you a particular set of instructions as well. Can you tell us what he asked of you?

**ANNIE:** Yes. Holmes came to me privately and told me that he wished me to go to Percy's room — the corner room — and to remain there. He was very specific: I was to sit in that room and I was not to leave it, for any reason, until he returned. He did not tell me why. He simply said that it was important, that I should trust him, and that under no circumstances was I to stir from the room. I agreed, of course. There was something in the way he said it that made one feel that compliance was not merely advisable but necessary.

**WATSON:** That is entirely characteristic of Holmes. He distributes instructions with perfect precision and almost no explanation. Each person is told exactly what they need to know and nothing more.

**SMITH:** Miss Harrison, how long did you wait in that room?

**ANNIE:** Some hours, I think, though I could not say with precision. It was a strange vigil. I sat in the corner room, in the dim light, not knowing what I was waiting for or whether anything would happen at all. The house was quiet. I began to wonder whether Holmes had been mistaken, or whether the entire exercise was a precaution that would prove unnecessary. And then Holmes himself appeared.

**SMITH:** He came to relieve you?

**ANNIE:** Yes. He came into the room quietly, later in the evening, and told me that he would take my place. He thanked me for keeping my post and asked me to go to my own room and remain there. Again, no explanation. I did as I was told.

**DOYLE:** When Watson gave me this account, it struck me as one of Holmes's most carefully staged operations. He had removed everyone whose presence might disturb the scene — Percy and Watson to London, Miss Harrison to her own room — and then installed himself alone in the corner room to wait. He had set the stage and taken his position in the wings.

**SMITH:** And sure enough, someone came. Mr. Phelps, you learned afterwards what happened that night in your room. Tell us what Holmes reported.

**PHELPS:** Holmes told us that an intruder did indeed enter the room. He came in the night — came, I should say, with the apparent confidence of someone who knew exactly where he was going and what he was after. He went to a particular spot and produced the treaty from its hiding place. Holmes watched him do it. He allowed the man to reveal where the document had been concealed, which was itself the critical intelligence Holmes needed, and then he moved to apprehend him.

**WATSON:** Holmes told me that the man was quick and that the struggle was brief. He got away — slipped out before Holmes could secure him. But Holmes had already seen what he needed to see, and he had the treaty in hand. The man had revealed himself and revealed the hiding place, and then was gone into the night. Holmes let him go rather than sacrifice the document.

**SMITH:** And who was this intruder? Miss Harrison, this is perhaps the most difficult part of this evening's conversation. The man who came for the treaty that night was your brother, Joseph Harrison.

**ANNIE:** Yes. It was Joseph. I will not pretend otherwise — it has been printed in Watson's account and it cannot be unmade. Joseph had been at the Foreign Office that night, as it happened; he was there to meet me, as I had sometimes visited Percy in the evenings. He had been in the building, he had seen the treaty lying on Percy's table, and he had understood — Joseph was not without intelligence in these matters — something of what it was and what it might be worth to certain interested parties. He seized the opportunity. When Percy left the room to answer that bell — a bell which Joseph himself had rung to draw Percy away — he took the document.

**PHELPS:** The bell. I have thought about that bell a hundred times. It seemed so inexplicable — I went to the door and found no one. I could not understand it at the time. It was only when Holmes explained it afterward that the whole chain became clear. Joseph rang the bell to empty the room, took the treaty in the minute I was absent, and then concealed it. He had been holding it at Briarbrae all along — in the very house where I lay ill.

**WATSON:** Which is a remarkable — one might almost say audacious — piece of concealment. The treaty was, in effect, hidden in plain sight. The very place where Percy was searching his memory and wearing himself to a shadow was the place where the document was secreted.

**ANNIE:** I knew nothing of it. I want to make that clear, though I understand perfectly well that no one can compel belief on such a point. I nursed Percy all those weeks in complete ignorance of what Joseph had done. The cruelty of it — the cruelty to Percy, and to me — is something I have had to make my peace with, and I shall not say that peace has come easily.

**SMITH:** Miss Harrison, no one here questions your integrity, and Watson's account is quite clear on that point. Mr. Phelps, Holmes brought the treaty safely back to London and presented it the following morning — at the breakfast table, I believe?

**PHELPS:** Yes. We had returned from London that morning — Watson and I — and Holmes was already there, in perfectly good spirits, as though nothing of great moment had occurred. We sat down to breakfast, and Holmes, when the covers were lifted from the dishes, revealed the treaty beneath one of them. I cannot adequately describe what I felt. All those weeks of illness and despair — and there it was. Recovered. I wept. I am not ashamed to say it. I wept at the breakfast table in front of everyone.

**WATSON:** It was one of the most extraordinary moments I have ever witnessed. Holmes had a gift for the theatrical, and on that morning he deployed it to full effect. The relief on Percy's face was something I shall not forget.

**SMITH:** Inspector Forbes, were you present for the resolution?

**FORBES:** I was not present at the breakfast, no. I was informed of the outcome afterwards and was, I confess, very interested to understand how Holmes had arrived at Joseph Harrison as his principal suspect, and how he had arranged matters so precisely. The treaty had been in that house for nine weeks without our knowing it. That is a fact which does not reflect entirely well on the official inquiry, and I say so without evasion. Holmes saw where we had not looked.

**DOYLE:** When Watson brought me this account, I was struck by what I can only call the human weight of it. It was not merely a theft of State papers — it was the story of a man's career and illness, a woman's faithfulness, and a betrayal lodged at the very heart of the household where the victim lay recovering. All of that had to live in the narrative alongside the detection itself.

**SMITH:** Miss Harrison, you have been very gracious in coming here today. Is there anything you wish to say about what followed the resolution?

**ANNIE:** Only that Percy recovered — fully recovered, in time — and that his good name was restored, and that Lord Holdhurst was satisfied. Those were the things that mattered. What Joseph did was his own doing and his own burden to carry. I could not undo it; I could only be certain that Percy knew I had no part in it. I believe he does know that.

**PHELPS:** Annie is more than generous. Throughout those nine weeks — through every sleepless night and every hopeless morning — she was there. She had no knowledge of what her brother had done. She was my nurse and my comfort and, in every sense that matters, my salvation. I owe her everything.

**SMITH:** Mr. Phelps, in hindsight, looking back at the entirety of the affair — is there anything you understand now that you did not understand then?

**PHELPS:** A great deal. I understand now how Holmes's mind worked in approaching the problem — the systematic way in which he established who could have known what, and when. At the time I was too deep in my own suffering to think clearly about anything. But I can see, looking back, the logic of his approach. He asked questions that seemed to me beside the point, but nothing was beside the point with Holmes. Every detail contributed to the whole.

**WATSON:** Holmes told me, I remember, that he preferred not to form conclusions without data. He said it more than once over the years — that it was a capital mistake to theorize without sufficient information. In the case of the treaty, he gathered his data with great care before committing to any line of action.

**DOYLE:** That discipline is one of the things that makes him so effective as a character — and, I trust, as a real investigator. The refusal to leap. The willingness to hold the problem open until the evidence speaks clearly.

**SMITH:** Inspector Forbes, a broader question, if you will: does the outcome of the naval treaty case change anything in how you approach your work — or in how Scotland Yard might approach similar investigations in the future?

**FORBES:** That is a fair question and I shall answer it fairly. The case demonstrated that the circle of suspicion, in an affair of this nature, can extend in unexpected directions. We at Scotland Yard proceeded along the most obvious lines — the official premises, the known personnel, those who were demonstrably on the spot. Holmes looked beyond the office entirely and examined the domestic situation of those connected with Mr. Phelps. That proved to be the decisive step. I would not say it is a lesson that Scotland Yard ignores entirely — we do consider the wider circle. But the single-mindedness with which Holmes pursued that particular thread was something I found instructive, however uncomfortable the process.

**WATSON:** He had a way of seeing the thing whole — the personal circumstances, the professional setting, the timing — all at once, and of following whichever strand seemed most alive. In this case it was the domestic strand, and he was right.

**SMITH:** We are nearly at the close of our time this evening, but I should like to ask each of you one final question. If you were to say what this case means to you — not what happened, but what it means, what you take from it — what would you say? Mr. Phelps, let us begin with you.

**PHELPS:** That a man's life is not over when it appears to be over. I was convinced, lying in that room at Briarbrae, that everything was finished — my career, my reputation, my future. Holmes recovered the treaty; Lord Holdhurst was satisfied; and I was given back what I had thought was lost irretrievably. I am aware that this is not always how matters resolve themselves in real life. But in this case, it did. And I have tried not to forget that when things seemed most hopeless, help was still possible.

**ANNIE:** That faithfulness in the dark days is not wasted. I did not know, during those weeks of nursing Percy, whether the treaty would ever be found or whether his name could ever be cleared. I only knew that he needed care, and that I could provide it. What the experience means to me is simply that — that one does what one can, and that it may, in the end, be sufficient.

**FORBES:** For me — and I say this as a professional who is not much given to sentiment — the case is a reminder of the value of admitting when one has reached the limit of one's own methods. I am not sure I acted on that realisation quickly enough at the time. But I know it now. When an investigation has reached a wall, the honest thing is to recognise the wall and to seek out whoever is best placed to see beyond it.

**WATSON:** For me, this case has always had a particular warmth because of my connection with Percy. He was my schoolfellow — Tadpole Phelps, we called him — and to see him brought so low and then so thoroughly restored was something that affected me as a friend more than as an observer. I have chronicled many of Holmes's cases and I shall continue to do so. But this one I feel in a different part of myself. I feel it as a man who was glad that an old friend came through.

**DOYLE:** And for me — writing these stories is, at its best, an act of faith in the idea that reason and perseverance can prevail over disorder and confusion. Holmes cannot always win; the world is not always so obliging. But in this case he did win, and the win mattered — for Mr. Phelps, for Miss Harrison, for the Foreign Office, and perhaps even for the broader security of England. When I sit down with Watson's notes, I sometimes feel the weight of the real stakes behind the narrative. In this case, that weight was very great.

**SMITH:** On behalf of *The Strand Magazine*, allow me to thank our guests — Mr. Percy Phelps, Miss Annie Harrison, and Inspector Forbes of Scotland Yard — for their willingness to revisit what must at times have been a difficult chapter of their experience. My gratitude, as always, to Arthur Conan Doyle and to Dr. John H. Watson, without whom these evenings would have no foundation. Ladies and gentlemen, this concludes the twenty-fifth seminar of our series. Good evening.

*Sustained applause*

# The Final Problem

*First Published in December, 1893*
*Sponsored by The Strand Magazine*
*Meeting Room B, British Museum, London*

**The Twenty-Sixth Seminar**

**Herbert Greenhough Smith** — The Strand Editor & Moderator
**Arthur Conan Doyle** — Author and Watson's Literary Agent
**Dr. John H. Watson** —Colleague and Biographer of Sherlock Holmes

Seminar Transcript

**SMITH:** Ladies and gentlemen, welcome once more to the British Museum, and to what is, I confess, the most solemn occasion in this series of commemorative seminars. We have arrived, after five and twenty preceding conversations, at the story which the reading public received in December of eighteen ninety-three — and which provoked, in this editor's memory, more letters of protest and grief than any other publication in the history of this magazine. I refer, of course, to "The Final Problem." With me today are Arthur Conan Doyle, who composed the narrative, and Dr. John H. Watson, who furnished the original case notes and who appears as the principal witness to the events described. There are no invited guest participants for today's proceedings, for the particular reason that the central figure of these events left no voice behind him to speak in this room. Gentlemen, welcome, and thank you both for being here.

**DOYLE:** Thank you, Smith. I will say, even now, that sitting here to discuss this particular story is not an easy matter. It is the ending of something, and endings are never wholly comfortable.

**WATSON:** For my part, I have thought carefully about whether to participate today. The events described in that story are not merely literary events to me. They are the most painful chapter of my life. But I agreed to come because Holmes himself was a man who valued the plain truth above sentiment, and I think he would have wanted the record to be as clear and as honest as possible.

**SMITH:** Dr. Watson, let us begin at the very beginning of the account. The story opens with your assertion that you had said nothing of the matter for three years — that you had kept silent out of respect for certain interests. Can you speak to that restraint?

**WATSON:** I can. When I came to set down these notes and pass them to Doyle, I was mindful that certain legal proceedings had not yet run their full course. Holmes had done a great deal of work, over several months, to assist the police in exposing the criminal organization over which Professor Moriarty presided. That organization was vast, and its dismantlement was not completed in a single day. I did not wish anything I wrote to compromise those efforts or to endanger persons who had cooperated with Holmes in confidence. By the time I did speak, I felt the interests that had required my silence were no longer in peril.

**SMITH:** Arthur, when Watson's notes reached you, was the decision to delay publication part of what he communicated to you?

**DOYLE:** It was. Watson was quite explicit on that point. He impressed upon me that if certain names and connections were published too soon, it could cause them harm. I respected that entirely. When the story did come to be written, I endeavored to stay true to the notes while exercising the usual writer's discretion about which details to emphasize. Though I will say, in this particular case, the notes themselves had a quality of emotional directness that I found I could not improve upon. Watson writes simply when he is in earnest.

**WATSON:** That is a generous thing to say.

**SMITH:** Dr. Watson, the story begins with Holmes arriving at your consulting rooms in a state of considerable agitation — quite unlike his usual composure. Can you describe that first visit, and the impression it made upon you?

**WATSON:** I had rarely seen Holmes in such a condition. He moved with a kind of restless vigilance — he examined the windows, drew the blind, and only then permitted himself to sit. He explained that he had been shadowed on his way to my rooms, that he had taken an extraordinary series of precautions to lose his pursuer, passing through a passage at the back of Cavendish Square, stopping at a carriage as if to enter it, and ultimately reaching my door by way of a circuitous path through streets and yards. What struck me most was not the agitation itself, but the cause he named. He had not, in all the years of our acquaintance, ever spoken to me about Professor Moriarty.

**SMITH:** And yet it was immediately plain to you that Moriarty was no ordinary subject?

**WATSON:** Holmes described him with a precision and a gravity that I had not heard him apply to any other adversary. He called Moriarty the Napoleon of Crime — a man who stood at the centre of a web that reached into every corner of criminal life in London, indeed in England, and yet whose own hands remained, to all appearances, entirely clean. Holmes told me that Moriarty was a man of good birth and exceptional intellect, a former Professor of Mathematics who had written a treatise on the Binomial Theorem and a work called 'The Dynamics of an Asteroid' — a book, Holmes said, that ascended to such rarefied heights of pure mathematics that there was no man in the scientific press capable of criticizing it.

**SMITH:** Arthur, it must have been a considerable challenge to render that portrait on the page — to convey a man whose crimes were never witnessed directly by Watson.

**DOYLE:** It was, in fact, one of the more interesting compositional problems the story presented. Watson had never met Moriarty at the time Holmes first described him to him, and so his notes necessarily relied upon what Holmes had told him. I had to trust in the power of Holmes's own characterization — the image of the spider at the centre of a web, of a man who was never himself present at the scene of any crime, who organized and directed and yet appeared always elsewhere. Holmes had the gift, which Watson captured, of making you feel the presence of a thing even in its absence.

**WATSON:** And yet I did see him, once, and briefly. He came to Baker Street. That same evening, after Holmes had spoken to me and I had returned home, Holmes sent me a note, and I went to him. He told me that Moriarty had called upon him in his rooms that very day. I did not see Moriarty on that occasion, but Holmes described the encounter in terms that I found deeply unsettling. A tall man — clean-shaven, pale, with deeply sunken eyes and a face that oscillated from side to side in a curiously reptilian fashion. He had come to warn Holmes off. To tell him plainly that his campaign to expose the organization must cease, or he, Moriarty, would find means to destroy him.

**SMITH:** Holmes did not yield to that warning.

**WATSON:** He had no intention of yielding. He told me that he had already been at work for three months, in close cooperation with the police. He asked me to remain in my rooms that night, to take precautions, and to accompany him to the Continent the following Monday morning.

**SMITH:** Let us speak about the departure itself. You left on Monday morning, the twenty-fourth of April. The arrangements were, I gather, elaborate.

**WATSON:** Very much so. Holmes had evidently been awake through the night making preparations. He did not want us seen leaving together from Victoria Station — he had observed one of Moriarty's men watching the approaches there. He sent me in a cab to Victoria, with specific instructions about the route to take and precautions to observe, but arranged that we would not travel from Victoria after all. At the last moment I was met by an elderly Italian priest in the compartment of the train who, once the train had moved and we were clear, revealed himself to be Holmes. He had disguised himself completely. We left the train at Canterbury, having given the impression to any watcher that we were bound for Dover and then for the Continent by the usual route. From Canterbury we made our way by another road to Newhaven, crossed to Dieppe, and so began our journey.

**SMITH:** Arthur, that scene of Holmes revealing himself as the priest — was that detail clearly present in Watson's notes?

**DOYLE:** It was, and it was a gift to any writer. The elderly Italian priest, entirely convincing, and then the quiet revelation once danger was past. What it tells you about Holmes is that even in the midst of what he knew to be the gravest danger he had ever faced, his theatrical instinct was wholly intact. He could not resist the performance.

**WATSON:** I confess I was both relieved and, for a moment, irritated. There had been genuine anxiety in those minutes on the platform. But he was right to take the precautions. As we learned later, Moriarty himself appeared at Victoria Station, having chartered a special train in an attempt to overtake us before we could cross. We did see him — we saw the special engine pass us at great speed as we stood watching from a bridge. Holmes remarked upon it with a kind of cold satisfaction. He said it was the last card Moriarty had to play on English soil, and that we were safe beyond the Channel.

**SMITH:** And for a time, you were.

**WATSON:** For a time. We spent several pleasant days on the Continent. We passed through Brussels, through Strasbourg, through Geneva. We wandered through the Rhône valley and the Bernese Oberland. Holmes seemed, during those days, almost at ease. He spoke about his work, about the cases that had interested him most, about his plans for what he called his magnum opus — a work in which he intended to set out his whole art of detection from first principles. It was during those weeks that I had some of my most candid conversations with him about the methods that had always seemed to me almost magical.

**SMITH:** And yet that interlude could not last.

**WATSON:** No. I noticed as we approached Switzerland that his manner changed. He became watchful again, quieter. I did not press him for an explanation, but on the third of May, as we came to the neighborhood of Meiringen, I had the sense that something had been decided, or that some message had reached him, though I cannot be certain of that. We were staying at the Englischer Hof, kept by a man named Peter Steiler the elder, who spoke excellent English, having spent three years as a waiter at the Grosvenor Hotel in London.

**SMITH:** It was Steiler who recommended the Reichenbach Falls to you.

**WATSON:** It was. He described them as well worth seeing, and that was perfectly true. I had not visited them before and I was glad of the recommendation on that account alone. Holmes agreed to go. We set out on what I supposed was simply a pleasant excursion. The falls are approached along a steep and narrow path, and they are a remarkable sight — a boiling, seething torrent of green water, the spray rising up like smoke from a burning building, the noise tremendous. We stood on a projecting rock that overlooked the abyss and looked down into it. It was a dreadful place. I remember thinking so even before I had reason to think worse of it.

**SMITH:** And then came the note.

**WATSON:** A boy from the hotel came running up the path to find me. He carried a note that purported to be from Steiler himself, written on the hotel's paper. It said that an English lady had arrived at the hotel in the last stages of consumption, in great distress, and that she had asked urgently whether there was an English doctor among the guests. Steiler, knowing I was a medical man, wrote asking me to return at once. It said that Holmes could perfectly well remain at the falls and that I could return to him afterwards or meet him at Rosenlaui where we were to spend the night.

**SMITH:** You went.

**WATSON:** I am not certain that I should not have taken Holmes with me regardless of what the note said. But at the time it seemed entirely plausible — the note was on the hotel's paper, the situation it described was one I had encountered before in practice, and an English patient in a strange country has a claim on an English doctor that is difficult to deny. Holmes himself urged me to go. That was the last time I spoke with him. I looked back once, from a turn in the path, and saw him standing at the lip of the abyss with his arms folded, watching me. I have thought of that image a great many times since.

**SMITH:** Arthur, how did you approach the writing of that moment?

**DOYLE:** It is one of the most important moments in the whole of Watson's notes, precisely because of its simplicity. Watson did not know, in that instant, that he was saying farewell. He looked back and saw a figure standing alone above an abyss, and then he walked on. To describe it plainly, as he did, is more powerful than any embellishment. I did not alter it. I could not have improved it.

**SMITH:** Dr. Watson, what did you find when you arrived at the hotel?

**WATSON:** Nothing. No English lady. No consumptive guest. Steiler had written no such note. He knew nothing of it. I realised at once that the note was a forgery, a device to separate me from Holmes, and I turned and ran back to the falls without waiting another moment. But I already knew, in some part of my mind that I did not want to listen to, what I was going to find.

**SMITH:** And what did you find?

**WATSON:** The path was empty. Holmes was not there. His alpenstock was leaning against a rock near the lip of the abyss, as though he had set it down for a moment. In the soft earth at the very edge, there were traces — footprints, two sets of them, leading to the brink. None leading away. I searched the whole of that path. I called out. I waited. There was no reply but the noise of the falls.

**SMITH:** And then you found the letter.

**WATSON:** Yes, Holmes had left a letter. It was placed upon a rock, weighted by his alpenstock, inside his cigarette case. He addressed it to me, and I happened to have brought it with me. With your permission, I will read it for the benefit of the audience:

*'My Dear Watson, I write these few lines through the courtesy of Mr. Moriarty, who awaits my convenience for the final discussion of those questions which lie between us. He has been giving me a sketch of the methods by which he avoided the English police and kept himself informed of our movements. They certainly confirm the very high opinion which I had formed of his abilities. I am pleased to think that I shall be able to free society from any further effects of his presence, though I fear that it is at a cost which will give pain to my friends, and especially, my dear Watson, to you. I have already explained to you, however, that my career had in any case reached its crisis, and that no possible conclusion to it could be more congenial to me than this. Indeed, if I may make a full confession to you, I was quite convinced that the letter from Meiringen was a hoax, and I allowed you to depart on that errand under the persuasion that some development of this sort would follow. Tell Inspector Patterson that the papers which he needs to convict the gang are in pigeon-hole M., done up in a blue envelope and inscribed 'Moriarty'. I made every disposition of my property before leaving England, and handed it to my brother Mycroft. Pray give my greetings to Mrs. Watson, and believe me to be, my dear fellow, Very sincerely yours, Sherlock Holmes."*

That letter is one of my most prized possessions. I immediately allowed the police to copy it, but I retain the original.

**DOYLE:** It's really quite a remarkable letter, and I want to thank you for reading it to us. As you know, I included it word for word in the written account, because I felt it to be last words of the greatest detective the world has ever known.

**SMITH:** Indeed. Arthur, it falls to me to ask the question that the reading public has not ceased to ask since December of eighteen ninety-three. The decision to end the story as you did, with Holmes apparently dead — was that fully your decision?

**DOYLE:** I would ask Watson's pardon before I answer. Watson, I think you know that the answer to that is yes and no, and that the full truth of it is not a simple matter. The notes Watson gave me ended precisely where the story ends. There was nothing beyond the edge of that precipice that Watson himself could attest to. He had not been there. What I had before me was the alpenstock, the footprints, the empty path, and the contents of his letter. I will say this: I was persuaded that the story of Sherlock Holmes had reached its natural end. A man who has spent his life in the pursuit of a single great adversary, and who destroys that adversary at the cost of his own life, has completed the work he was made for.

**WATSON:** I find I cannot argue with that on intellectual grounds. And yet I will say, with your permission, that there is something which I have never been fully at ease with. In my opinion, the note Holmes left was not the language of a man who felt that everything had been said and done.

**SMITH:** Gentlemen, you are touching on something that I suspect this audience finds particularly compelling — the question of what Holmes himself believed he was going to. Did he expect to survive?

**WATSON:** His note suggests he did not expect to survive. But that is not the same as believing he could not. Holmes was not, in my experience, a man who accepted defeat as inevitable merely because the odds were very long. He was a man who accepted facts as facts, and who acted upon his best assessment of them. I believe he went to the edge of that cliff knowing that Moriarty would come, knowing that the struggle would be mortal, and prepared to die if that was the cost. Whether he judged that cost acceptable is another question. I believe he did.

**DOYLE:** And that, I think, is the whole meaning of the story. Holmes had, by his own account, identified and exposed the central criminal intelligence of England. The organization that had, as he told Watson, made one hundred and twenty-three separate crimes possible in the previous twelve months — this organization had been broken. Holmes knew, when he stood at Reichenbach Falls, that the arrests were made, that the evidence was secure, that the work was done. He was not sacrificing himself for a doubtful cause. He was paying the final price of a victory that was already certain.

**SMITH:** Dr. Watson, because you were with Holmes, you were yourself subjected to no small danger during those days. You might easily not have survived to reach Switzerland at all.

**WATSON:** That is true, and Holmes acknowledged it. He was troubled by the danger to which he had exposed me, more than he liked to show. But I want to be clear that I did not accompany him under any misapprehension. He told me plainly that our journey was not without risk. He asked for my company because he trusted me, and because he felt, I think, that a man facing what he faced should not face it entirely alone. I would not have missed being with him during those weeks for anything that I know of in this world.

**SMITH:** Arthur, as the man who wrote the story, looking back upon it from the distance of seven years — what is it that you believe the story finally says?

**DOYLE:** I believe it says that there are some men who are formed for great and singular purposes, and who are used by those purposes as completely as a strong fire uses its fuel. Holmes was such a man. He was not made for ordinary life — not for comfort, nor for rest, nor for the small daily satisfactions that sustain most of us. He was made for the particular contest that his life had set before him. And when that contest reached its climax, he met it without flinching. The story says that such a meeting, at such a place, at such a cost, is not a defeat. It may even be, in its fashion, a kind of completion.

**WATSON:** I think that is true. I have not always found it easy to believe, but I think it is true. Holmes would have said that the calculation was straightforward. One life, against the destruction of an organization responsible for the misery and ruin of a great many lives. He would have found it perfectly obvious which way that calculation must fall.

**SMITH:** And yet you dispute it, Dr. Watson, just a little.

**WATSON:** I dispute the ease of it. I do not dispute the logic. A man may be both correct in his reasoning and deeply lamented by those who loved him. I do not think Holmes would have found anything irrational in that.

**SMITH:** One final matter, if I may. The story, as published, closes with a brief reference to the attempts of Colonel James Moriarty to rehabilitate his brother's reputation in the press — to contest the account that had been given of the Professor's criminal character. Watson, you referred to this in the narrative. What was your view of those attempts?

**WATSON:** My view was and remains that they were without foundation. Holmes had spent three months in the most painstaking investigation, had assembled evidence of overwhelming force, and had placed that evidence before the police authorities. The arrests that were made in the days following our departure confirmed everything that Holmes had described. The organization was real, the crimes were real, and the Professor's direction of them was established beyond any reasonable contest. Colonel Moriarty's letters to the press were the natural, understandable, and entirely mistaken expressions of a brother's grief. They do not alter a single fact.

**DOYLE:** And I think it is worth remarking, for the benefit of those present, that Watson's choice to mention those letters at all speaks well of his character. He did not ignore the challenge to the account. He acknowledged it, refuted it, and moved on. That is the method of a fair-minded man.

**SMITH:** Gentlemen, I am conscious that this has been the longest and, in some respects, the most difficult of these seminars. We have discussed a story that ends with loss rather than resolution, with grief rather than vindication — or rather, with a vindication that cannot fully console the man who must live with its cost. I want to thank you both, not only for the thoroughness and honesty of your answers today, but for the patience with which you have engaged with questions that are, I think we must all acknowledge, not merely literary questions. Dr. Watson, the friendship you bore Mr. Holmes, and the fidelity with which you have preserved and communicated the record of his work, are themselves a kind of monument. Arthur, the story you shaped from Watson's notes has moved and will continue to move a great many people who never knew Holmes at all, and that is no small thing.

**WATSON:** Thank you, Mr. Smith. I am grateful for the opportunity to speak plainly about it. Holmes would not have wanted silence.

**DOYLE:** On that point, Dr. Watson, I think we are entirely in agreement. Ladies and gentlemen, this concludes the twenty-sixth and final seminar of The Strand Magazine's Commemorative Series. Good day.

*Sustained applause*

# About the Author

Thomas "Tom" Campbell is a Wilmington, North Carolina resident who shares his home with his dog, Watson. His diverse professional career has spanned multiple industries, including his role as an Account Executive - Industry Consultant with AT&T Information Systems. Tom has also demonstrated his entrepreneurial spirit by operating Beach PC, a local computer repair business, and serving as owner/operator of Advanced Legal Software, a statewide company that specialized in family law applications.

Beyond his professional pursuits, Tom maintains an active personal life centered around his community and interests. He is a dedicated member of the Sherlock Holmes Society of the Cape Fear, serves as a Sunday school teacher at the First Baptist Church of Carolina Beach, and treasures time spent on family vacations.

Tom can be reached through the Sherlockian website listed below:

**www.SherlockHolmesSociety.com**

www.ingramcontent.com/pod-product-compliance
Lightning Source LLC
LaVergne TN
LVHW010621100826
845148LV00014B/3056

* 9 7 9 8 2 3 4 0 5 5 3 5 4 *